TRACKING JULIE STENSVAHL

By Bill Wehner

One More Chapter Publishing
Modesto, CA

Cover Art by Linda Werner

ISBN: 978-1-935252-54-2
© 2011 Bill Wehner

Published By: *One More Chapter Publishing*

Author's Note:

The usual author's liberties have been taken; this after all, is a novel, a figment of the author's imagination. The author (that's me) does not mean to portray any person, living or dead, in this book. That doesn't mean that the author has not stolen liberally from his life acquaintances and experience. Nor is this book intended to be an accurate portrayal of the US Forest Service or any government agency. While the book is based on the author's experience with the Gila, Blue and Aldo Leopold Wilderness Areas of New Mexico, the Mimbres Wilderness exists only, as does the rest of the book, in the imagination of the author.

Bill Wehner
Columbus NM,
December 1st, 2010

wehner@vtc.net

Dedication

This effort is dedicated to Tom Bridge and to 'Armie' Armbruster; both died too soon.

Acknowledgements

This little book could not have been written without the help of my biggest fan and severest critic, my wife Mary. Neighbor Mirs Satran was kind enough to read the manuscript and loan me his tracking and firearms expertise. Debbi Evans is the kind of proofreader every author dreams about and has earned my undying thanks. Robert Odom kind of started the ball rolling, then proofed my Spanish without laughing out loud; Paul Salopek, Carol Coats, Susan Wehner, and Tom Willmott read the manuscript and offered nothing but encouragement. Every budding author should have friends like these.

Linda Werner is the artist who found the time to paint the cover in spite of her duties as the Columbus Head Librarian. And I probably should mention Paula Rapp Hall, who was inadvertently responsible for the creation of Eddie Sam and John Henry Clay.

Contents

Prologue

The small man liked to think he moved like a ghost along the ridge, careful not to skyline himself. An Apache ghost. He prided himself in his skills in these wooded mountains. The cover up here was not heavy - mostly pinon and juniper, but the going was extremely tough. Below him on the stream bottoms it was rougher, even on the few game trails. At least here there was no thick brush to impede his way; a few dense clumps of evergreen, but for the most part the trees kept a discrete distance from one another. Tight enough to screen his route from below but very exposed from above, if someone were in a helicopter, he thought. The ridge itself was littered with irregular dark red boulders, from the size of a Volkswagen down to a shoebox; the gravel underfoot was the same red. Lichens, mostly gray but with a sampling of yellows and blues, matted most of the larger rocks. Scattered here and there among the evergreens were low clumps of sad looking prickly pear and an occasional dismal cholla. At best it was slow going, even for a ghost, he decided.

He wore Cabela's best hiking boots; had on cargo-style hunting trousers in Aspen Break-up Camo, and a flannel shirt under his grimy buckskin jacket. He had a fanny pack/utility belt that included among other things a 7" Buck knife, a comb and a pouch containing .30-30 rounds for the Winchester '94 Saddle Ring (with the ring removed) Carbine he carried in his left hand. The fanny pack held a small Bible, a handful of beef jerky, and a small plastic sack containing dryer lint. In his left ear was a radio bud that so far had produced nothing, not even static. Even though he knew he had been saving the batteries of the tiny Midland radio, a shade of doubt ran through his mind.

He appeared rather slight at first glance, but the broad shoulders would be immediately noted. He was clean shaven and could have been 40 or even 35. While he would never admit to it, he was much closer to 50 than 40. Lank blonde hair was beginning to streak gray and he was showing a slight paunch in spite of close to a half year running around these damned mountains.

The early dawn was showing off the New Mexico sky for all it was worth, crimson and purple creeping over the Black Range in the near distance. He thought the day would be mostly clear except for some cirrus way up high; might even have a thunder shower before dark.

He was roughly paralleling a game trail about 200 meters to the east. A few minutes earlier he had observed two people – a middle aged man and a very young woman – on the trail, working carefully down hill, about 30 or 40 meters apart, the man in the lead. He had been keeping an occasional eye on them since they had shown up about 10 days earlier but hadn't quite settled on what they were doing in what he considered his personal country. They had camped on the bench overlooking No-Name Creek, near the pond. The man took off over the ridge back into the mountains most days while she fooled around their camp or explored some of the old pueblos on the cliff face. He had followed the man the first day but lost him within an hour. Besides, it was more fun shadowing the girl; she liked to sunbathe and would even occasionally strip to wash up in the pond. *My goodness,* he remembered, *how them nipples would stand up.*

Now it looked like they were on their way out. If they ran into his Relief Column, as he like to think of it, who knows what might happen, but it couldn't be helped. Most likely, nothing.

There was a click in his earbud, followed by another, then a voice: "...Orville?"

He double clicked the mike button in response. "Hey, Orville, we're about at the rendezvous, over."

"Alright, Luke, there a couple of hikers coming your way down slope, maybe 300 meters from the fork. Let 'em pass, no trouble, you hear?"

"Ten-four."

He had lost sight of the couple on the game trail, and he was still a minute or so short of the point where he could observe any trail activity below. But he didn't hurry, he had faith in his 'boys', his relief column. Then he heard a shout followed by bellowed words that he couldn't understand from the trail almost directly below him. A second or so later this was followed by a single shot, then two more. Almost immediately came answering fire – automatic fire – seemingly from a little further west. Three more spaced shots, then a volley of automatic fire and a girl's high pitched shriek. He plunged the last few steps to the overlook.

"(click)...fool fired on us...what the hell?...Orville?"

"Where are... I can't see you... anybody hurt?"

"Charlie took one in the calf; he's nicked but he says he can walk." Pause. "Ah...that nutcase is down... not moving."

Then, "(click)... (click)...Orville?" Then, "Shit, man there are guys coming down Black Run. We are moving out."

"Dammit Luke, drop the goods at Cairn Number One and get out of there. Who was firing the automatic rifle?"

"...ah... I got a Mini Uzi...ah, we're outta here, man."

And Elder Orville Foss stood overlooking the valley below him and glanced up to the sky. After a moment, he went to his knees, bowed his head and said, "Aw, shit!"

Day 1

The Call

John Henry Clay was a tidy man for someone his size, which in fact was a fraction over 6′ 8″. Beyond his library, he actually had few possessions. Accustomed for most of his adult life to moving on by tossing all his belongings into a foot locker and duffle bag, it wasn't hard to have a place for everything and to keep everything in its place, almost.

So it was a surprise when the phone rang, because he reached for it on the night stand where he always put it before retiring only to discover that it wasn't there. The realization came slowly: the cell phone had been knocked to the floor during the evening's activities, along with a scattering of small change and other odds and ends. He rummaged for it under the stray clothing on the floor. Finally, it came to hand. The screen showed 4:07 AM. It was not the ringing phone.

He staggered into the kitchen, fumbled for the light switch. The land line was on the counter, blinking furiously. "Lo."

"Mr. Clay? This is Dianne Stensvahl. Dub's ex. You remember?"

Dub Stensvahl. Good God, will I ever hear the last of him? "Yes ma'am, I remember you. What can I do for you?"

"Mr. Clay, I need your help. It's Dub. I don't know what to do." He heard her swallow a sob. "Dub's been shot. I'm at Silver City Memorial. He's asked for you. I think he's dying. They want to transport – medivac – him to Albuquerque if they can stabilize him. I don't know what to do."

"Ma'am, slow down... those folks are pretty good; they'll do the right thing."

"No, no, you don't understand. It's my daughter – she's up there somewhere..."

"Ma'am? What do you mean; what or where is 'somewhere'?" *Slow down and make some sense, lady.*

"I'm sorry." Her voice had lost some of its panic quality. "It's my daughter, Julie. She went up into the Mimbres with Dub last week. Some forest service people found him sometime today – I mean, yesterday, now – anyhow, she wasn't with him... Julie, I mean. I don't know whether she's been kidnapped, or if she's dead, or..." and she broke into sobs.

As she talked, he registered the gist of the story: Dub had somehow gotten himself shot; their daughter who had been with him was now missing; Dub's ex was scared to death.

Clay had her go over the story again. *Damn Dub anyhow!*

He hung up after the usual assurances. *Damn! It's the old "damsel in distress" thing again. Whatever Dub was up to, he probably deserved what happened. When will I learn to say no? She – make that they – want me to try to find their daughter. Find her in the Mimbres Wilderness...almost 200,000 acres, most of it above 7,000 feet, largely unexplored since the Black Range silver rush, Lord only knows how long ago that was- a hundred years? Was there only one established trail through it? I don't remember... it's been too long since I was up there... What the hell were they doing up there that got him shot? Not, come to think of it, that he probably didn't deserve it...*

The single-wide was a mess. He must have crapped out before she had even gone home. He wandered naked into the living room/kitchenette. Dirty dishes still on the table, empty wine bottle, shirt thrown into the corner of the sofa. *I hope she found all her stuff.* As bleary as he was, its condition still offended his sense of order and well being. Not that he was a neat freak – two ex-wives would be willing to testify to that. The stove was a mess, the table was a mess. *Well, my life's a mess.* He stacked the dirty dishes after rinsing them almost clean, dumped the empty bottle (a nice Cabernet, he noticed) into the trash, and was wiping down the stove when he stopped mid-stroke, and said aloud, "What the hell am I doing?" He walked back to the bedroom. He kicked the dirty clothing at the laundry basket, chanced a look at himself in the mirror. As always, he had to stoop slightly to get a full view of his face, the face of a tired man pushing 60 and showing it. He looked pretty bleary-eyed, his moustache askew from the pillow. *Am I hung over?* He asked himself. He'd had at least half that bottle of wine with dinner; *I guess I'll know sooner or later.* He decided not to shave, took a much needed shower and dried off with an old GI bath towel.

He put on khakis, a tee-shirt, and a long-sleeved tee-shirt over that. Both tees had pockets. He selected wool-blend socks and his New Balance hiking shoes. To his pack he added four tee-shirts and jockey shorts, two pairs of khakis, five pairs of socks, a pair of long johns, an extra sweat shirt, and bandanas. The rest of the pack was ready because he kept it that way; sleeping bag, open cell pad, ground cloth, toilet kit, pop-up mountain tent, single burner butane stove, collapsible camp stool (a two lb. luxury he granted himself and his aging knees) and rations for a week, plus the odds and ends that any backpacker considers he must have. Then, as an afterthought, he added another pair of socks. He slipped his reading glasses into the inner tee-shirt pocket, truck keys into his right pants pocket along with a Chapstick. By this time the coffee was brewed and he filled a thermos. His left pants pocket contained a butane lighter and a small imitation leather folder for license and credit cards. He was ready; *so what have I forgotten?*

"Oh," he said aloud, rummaged for the cell phone and dialed a familiar number. Although John Henry Clay would gleefully consign all cell phones to the deepest, darkest recesses of hell, he had to admit it had its uses.

A disembodied female voice answered after the third ring. "Hello, you have reached Frontera Tours, the Southwest's Premier Guide Service. Please leave a message; we will get back to you as soon as we can."

"Good morning, April, this is John Henry. I won't be around for a couple of days, but I don't think you had anything for me 'til next week, anyway. I'll give you a call when I get back." He noted that his phone seemed fully charged and dropped it in his pocket.

He thought about the evening before... was it just yesterday? He smiled, decided to think about it again, later.

Pulling his utility belt from the bedroom door hook, he unconsciously checked off the items clipped to it: small LED flashlight, Leatherman multi-tool, fanny pack first aid kit, and two small holsters- one for the .22 revolver he always carried in the woods, and the other for a bottle of Tabasco Sauce (Green Pepper). He added his beat-up E-tool to it along with a hunting knife – both of them he recalled, along with the cowboy 'stache, were souvenirs of Columbia – or was it Honduras? *The trick back then was to look as fearsome as you could,* he thought. *Well, he guessed he'd scare somebody now...*

Clay shucked into a hooded sweatshirt, found his old Celtics cap and carried the pack and utility belt to the truck. The morning had a chill in it, a reminder of things to come. When he returned to the mobile home for the coffee, he retrieved his ski jacket from the closet and took it to the truck as well. *If I don't have everything I need, I suppose I can pick it up in Silver,* he thought.

Alpine, Arizona

The four of them stomped into the Bear Paw Café, Alpine, Arizona's première and only restaurant, shaking off the early morning chill and trying to get circulation going again. The two Greenlee County deputies had arrived first followed a minute or two later by Martin Begay. As the three mounted the worn wooden steps of the eatery, Eddie Sam pulled up, stepped out of his pickup as though he owned the place, and hailed the other three, who waited with a show of feigned impatience. "Get your ass t'goin', Injun," the taller of the two deputies called out. He got a finger in reply.

As the waitress seated them, they all ordered coffee, three black and one double cream for Eddie. They made small talk, the deputy named Ray mostly yawned as they sipped slowly at their caffeine boost. None of the four had slept a great deal the past several nights. The sheriff's men were going off duty (at last); Begay wasn't crazy about sleeping on the ground and made no bones about it; and Eddie was just about walked-out. None of them had gotten to sleep before midnight following the FBI debriefing. It was several minutes before dawn when they had pulled out of the rendezvous at Hannagan Meadow, down on US 191.

Hagan had worked with Begay before, Ray knew. Eddie Sam was the newcomer. Ray sized up the man seated across from him; *tall for a Navajo, big shoulders, narrow hips, beginnings of a pot...about 45*, he guessed. *Short, spiky black hair, dark- could pass as a Mexican*, he thought.

Martin Begay, by contrast, was maybe 6 foot, thin, angular, black hair flecked gray pulled back in a short pony tail. He was older than Eddie Sam, perhaps 10 years? Begay tended to be bright and talkative, Sam could be silent for hours, then take a soapbox on almost anything. Interesting man.

Deputy Tim Hagan ordered the Alpine omelet special,

Eddie Sam ordered huevos rancheros, Ray said that he'd have the special too, and Eddie's cousin Martin ordered a Navajo taco. The others stared at him wide eyed.

"My god!" Tim Hagan made a gagging noise.

Eddie Sam said *yuck!* and turned his head away.

Begay was all wide-eyed innocence. "What?"

"What kind of breakfast is that?" Ray questioned, shaking his head.

"Hey, Bro, you goin' ethnic on us alluva sudden?" Eddie demanded. Martin just smiled the way he always did when the guys started ragging him.

Hagan said: "Enough to gag a maggot."

Martin grinned. "It's tough out there in those woods, boys. Some of us have to work for a living... you gringos wouldn't know a good stick-to-the-ribs breakfast if it kicked you in the ass."

Ray said, "Somebody ought t' kick you in the ass."

Hagan made as if to stand up. "Boys, we need to either change tables or throw him out."

The waitress had appeared with a fresh pot, "Alright, children, behave – or Aunty Jo will have you all throwed out," she said sweetly.

The food finally arrived and there was silence at the table, except for the somewhat theatrical slurping sounds that Martin made as he lingered over the fry bread taco.

"You think them dogs will turn up anything?"

"Tim, I'll tell you what... Those damn dogs didn't turn anything up the first time, they ain't gonna do it now," Eddie answered.

"I dunno," Ray put in, "I've watched that guy Bowman before, you remember, that hunt for a lost hiker over in the Chiricahua. He's pretty good. Says he learned his trade in Nam."

"You mean the dog's pretty good. Yeah, I watched him work Sadie, too. But if Orville ain't in there, Orville ain't in there!"

"How the hell do you know he ain't in there all snugged up in some hidey hole – just because you can't turn him up?"

Martin picked it up: "If Eddie says he ain't there, you can take it to the bank. What have we got to work on? His old truck parked out there near Horsehead Spring? A couple topo maps at his house? That man's an old fox. He's been to the mountain and he's been baptized. There'd be nobody better to lay a phony trail. He thinks he's Dan'l Boone, and he just might be. I don't think he was *ever* in there."

The two deputies had been working the manhunt for Elder Orville Foss for the last week along with 2 dozen other law enforcement people assigned to the Tucson FBI Office specifically for that purpose. All indications were that he had gone to ground in eastern Arizona's Blue Range Primitive Area, a part of the Apache National Forest. Eddie Sam and his cousin had been hired as contract trackers, and then yesterday had been pulled out to make way for the dogs. Martin had touted his cousin's talents to the District Ranger after he had gotten on the payroll himself. "Eddie Sam could track a flea across a Wally-World parking lot," he told him. A call to the Chiricahua produced a ranger's comment that "...Sam was the best intuitive tracker he'd ever watched work." That both trackers were not pleased about being displaced by a couple bloodhounds was abundantly clear.

Tim commented, "Well, if he *is* hiding out in there, winter's comin' on, he ain't going last through that. Where you boys headed from here?"

Eddie scowled, "Aw, we go back to the Reserve Ranger Station until we're 'redeployed', which means that the Feds will prob'ly be sending us back in a day or two, only this time I'm gonna bet they'll send us in from the New Mexico side. And, dammit, we still won't find anything."

Martin said, "That's alright, Hotshot, we'll still be on the government tit. Just doin' our job. Enjoy it while it lasts." That earned a snort of disgust from Eddie.

Ray said, "That pretty country over that way too. Once you're on the other side of Pueblo Creek, they ain't nothin' except some deer, a few elk and couple black bear."

"I've hunted up out of Pueblo Park. It's an old CCC camp in pretty good shape with decent outhouses. Up about 6,000 feet. No water though, it's a dry camp," Tim Hagan put in.

"Oh, screw you, anyway," to Martin, then to both deputies: "I've seen enough pretty country to last a day or two. My feet hurt. My back aches. I'm going to spend a couple days picking off ticks, and showering, and sleeping. I'm getting too old put up with this FBI crap. Every one of those suits knows better that we do, 'cause they all seen the same movies."

"All pays the same, Bro. Us Original Americans gotta keep the faith, keep the White Eyes off our poor achin' backs."

"Aw, get offa *my* back," Hagan replied, "I'm part Cherokee."

"I know, man, I know. I told you, I try not to hold it against you."

This last brought a guffaw from Ray, who said, "Let's get outa here, Tim. I can't hardly stand no more of these poor Injun tears. Yours included."

Hagan stood up. "You guys stay out of trouble, hear? You get down our way, to Clifton, drop in. Might even spring for a donut, who knows."

"Yeah, take care. Good to work with pros for a change." They shook hands around, paid their bills.

After the deputies headed back down 191 to their duty station, Eddie Sam leaned back against the tailgate of his truck, and thought, *That used to be Highway 666 'til the Bible thumpers bitched that it was the Devil's Number... Oh, well.* He eyed the thin overcast above them. "What the hell are we doing, Bro? Here we are trying to collar some poor shitkicker for what... knocking up some underage twat? There are hundreds – thousands – of illegals out there, maybe half of them lugging bad-assed drugs, and we got the Feebees tying up God knows how many good guys trying to catch this poor bastard. Is he more important than all the rest of this crap? I donno, man. I've just about had it."

"Eddie, Eddie... you *are* thinking too much again. You'll strain something. I gotta go fill up, I'm about outta gas." Then, "He's too slick for them anyways."

"I know, man. That's the whole trouble, isn't it."

"Massa, we jus' two guys tryin' to make a livin.' "

Silver City

John Henry Clay pulled up to the stop sign where North Boundary Street met State Highway 11, then turned north on 11 toward Deming, some 30 miles ahead. Before long there would be gray in the east, but no sign of it now. He slipped a Doc Watson disc into the player, heard the opening bars of *Greenville Trestle High,* eased down in the seat and sang along. He found his mind going back to Dub Stensvahl. Damn. Too much history there. He topped the rise at milepost 9 and the lights from the Border Patrol Check Point came into view at milepost 12. *Those boys are just waiting for the shift change*, he thought. *I wonder how much traffic they get here this time of morning?*

"Good morning, sir. US citizen?"

"Yessir."

"Where are you coming from?"

"Home. Columbus."

"And where are you headed, sir?"

"Silver."

A dog handler had made the circuit of Clay's pickup, and returned to the trailer that served as the BP outpost. The agent talking to Clay gave him a half salute, and said, "Have a good day, sir."

Yeah, a good day, thought John Henry. *I don't think I'd bet on that.*

John Henry Clay did not ordinarily consider himself an introspective man, but had to admit that he was given to accidental deep thought from time to time, especially when it involved a dawn awakening and a long drive. How many times had he tumbled to that 'damsel in distress' thing? He had at least one totally failed marriage he owed to that weakness. Clay did not consider himself a success at the game of life; he had been exposed to the Jesuits too long for that. Well... he had been an athlete who failed to make the bigtime. A couple years in the long-gone ABA... a career loser with the Washington Generals, wow... a season on an NBA taxi squad...

Almost was never good enough for Fr. Walter; it wasn't good enough for my dad, either, he thought. He'd been maybe good enough as a jungle warrior – that he was alive to think about it was proof enough, though he certainly could have been better at it. *Taking a bullet tends to demonstrate that.*

Dub Stensvahl. A brilliantly gifted basketball player. Dumped it all in the crapper. What a waste.

For some reason, he flashed on high school and Father Walter. *Didn't bother to tell me there were colleges with scholarship money interested in me until after I graduated. He thought that it would be a distraction to me...maybe it would have been...Why is this crap coming back after all these years?*

Coming up on milepost 16, John Henry became aware that he was being followed. He could barely make out the light rack on the roof of the vehicle tailing him. Since no one had been following him at the check station, he figured the cop – or maybe Border Patrol – had been stationed at someplace just beyond there.

What now?

When the light bar on the vehicle behind him began blinking its red, blue, red, blue – Clay pulled well over onto the berm, dug the document clip that contained his license out of his pocket, put both hands at the wheel top and waited. He had been going 65, just five over. Well, maybe it had been a slow shift for this guy.

The officer stopped just behind the open driver's window, flashlight beam in John Henry's face. "Mr. Clay," he said, "what are you doing up this early?"

Clay recognized the voice, and replied, "Goddammit, Roger, get that light out of my eyes." Luna County Deputy Roger Jeffers laughed, dropped the beam. "What the hell are you stopping me for, anyhow?"

"Why, John Henry, this is my day to go out into the world

and find folks to profile. Like hassling fat old Anglos with hair on their faces. Actually, John Henry, you've a taillight out on the right side. You know full well that if Poochie were to see that he'd have you locked up, drawn and quartered."

"I've fixed that stupid thing twice. I suppose that I could take it back to the dealer. Maybe his duct tape is better than mine."

"Chewing gum, works every time. What brings you out of your cozy cocoon so early? It's not like you greet the birds."

Jeffers was a stocky, medium sized man, one who probably who would not stand out in a crowd no matter where he was. He was some past middle age, having come to law enforcement late in life. While he didn't talk much about earlier careers, John Henry sensed there might have been a few parallels to his own, although probably not as a basketball player. He also was willing to bet that there were no other deputies in New Mexico with a doctorate in Comparative Religions. The only complaint he'd ever heard about Roger was that he consistently outscored the rest of the department on the pistol range.

A car passed, the first one he'd seen since leaving the check station. "I'll ask you the same thing, Roger. You guys short handed?" He knew that the deputy's normal duties had him on daytime patrol three days a week in the Columbus area, the other two around Deming, the county seat. It was a nine to five job that he guarded zealously.

"Busy night at the border. Two new citizens, and a firefight that almost ran the barricade. Had to medivac three banditos. At least two of them were still alive when they loaded them. I'm covering for Donnie and for Ed Cristman. And you, sir? Let's have your sad tale."

So John Henry told him what he knew. Then he asked, " You knew Dub... you know anything about why he decided to come back to the area? Seems like he skipped when Old Man Escalara tried to collect from him, or so they say." He didn't add, *and skipped with the $3500 I loaned him.*

"I don't know, John Henry. I'd heard he was back, oh, I suppose a few months ago. Maybe he decided to chance it when the Old Man died; maybe he figured that all would be forgiven – like the boys wouldn't remember." Then he added, "Stensvahl and you go back a way, don't you? Wasn't he a ball player, too?"

"Yeah... actually, a great talent squandered."

He watched Roger do a U-turn behind him, as he pulled back on to the highway. He poured another cup of coffee, turned Doc Watson back on, and thought about Dub Stensvahl. They had both played in the Big Ten. Stensvahl was a tall and rangy Minnesotan, had quick feet and sure hands. The quintessential small forward with a nice touch from 20 feet or so, brimming with talent and with an ego to match. They were separated in age by at least 15 years; it had been a few years since Clay had even played in a pick-up game. He wondered idly what kind of shape Dub kept himself in...

He was coming up on Deming now, so he eased off to a legal 55 as the first of the outlying businesses flashed by.

Well, this morning has certainly been interesting so far...what's that Chinese thing about living in interesting times...?

The fifty mile drive to Silver City from Deming is one without much interest to the casual observer. The Chihuahuan desert of scrub mesquite and creosote gradually rises almost 2000 feet in that fifty miles, crossing the usually dry Mimbres River a few miles out of Deming. The Mimbres winds down from the Black Range (a part of the Gila) and eventually disappears under the desert sand a few miles east of Deming, even when running bank-full as it does a few times a year. The upper end of the Mimbres waters a fertile valley year-round and supports a slew of agricultural enterprises on its banks.

This part of New Mexico is typified by sharp mountains rising from flat plains, some the result of subsidence and a great many formed by volcanic action. Most of the small southern ranges – Tres Hermanas, Floridas, and Hachitas, for instance, are at first glance barren. While they are for the most part without trees, they are anything but bare of growth, for the great sustainer of life, water, originates in the mountains and disappears into the deserts. Silver City is a small surprise when arriving from the south because, being a part of the great Gila chain, it is green. There are trees.

The change from flat desert land to bajadas and foothills is subtle. Suddenly, one is in the high mountains where, unlike the smaller ranges, greenery in the form of trees abounds. Ponderosa and pinon pines, common and alligator juniper form an ecology base for some of America's most primitive areas – the Leopold, Mimbres, Blue and Gila Wilderness Areas.

Dub Stensvahl

They met in the hospital cafeteria. Clay had another cup of coffee, Dianne Stensvahl teased a tea bag in a cup of hot water. The smell of food reminded him that a trail bar had been his only breakfast this morning.

"Miz Stensvahl, I'm sorry for your trouble. I hate to drag you back over it but I need the whole story from the beginning if you don't mind."

"Please, Mr. Clay... Dianne."

"Yes, ma'am, but you will have to call me John Henry. It's hard for me to answer to 'Mr. Clay.'"

Dianne Stensvahl was pretty much the way he remembered her, he thought. Tall, big-boned woman in jeans and pink sweat shirt, running shoes; pink sweatband holding her hair in place. Still attractive at forty, no doubt about it.

"Ah... I got a call last evening that they'd brought Dub in. He was in surgery a good part of the night. Right now they are trying to decide whether he's still bleeding internally."

"Do you know anything about the shooting itself?"

"Only what the deputies told me. I guess Dub was ambushed. He told them three men..."

"Yes ma'am. You mentioned your daughter. How is she involved?"

"About 10 days ago, Dub showed up, wanting to take Julie with him on a back country hike. I didn't like it very much, especially with her starting basketball practice, and with school and all. He said that it would be the last chance this season, and besides, she was growing up and they wouldn't have many more chances. I still thought it would be a lousy idea, but Julie begged me; besides he hasn't spent much time with her the last year or two and she idolizes him. I think you know how charming that son-of-a-bitch can be when he wants to. Anyway, she's an experienced hiker and camper, so in the end I said yes."

"Tell me about her."

"She's a good girl... just started her sophomore year. Julie's a big girl, 6 feet and still growing...she's good at basketball; she and her dad used to play against each other when he was around. They started doing that again a few months ago. She is a 'B' student, mostly... doesn't have much to do with boys... her one big enthusiasm is basketball. Maybe partly because of Dub, but I think Julie would have gotten involved in it no matter."

"What about Dub? When did he come back? I'd heard he had left for good – wasn't ever gonna come back to New Mexico."

"He showed up again about five months ago, said he'd been spending a lot of time up around the Black Range; and he looked good, like he'd spent a lot of time out-doors. He'd be around for several days, then we wouldn't see him for a week, then he'd just be hanging around again and he and Julie would go off to the gym together."

"How did you happen to call me?" he asked.

"Ah... I guess I didn't know who else to call. I knew that the two of you had worked together a few years ago... I asked the deputy who interviewed me if he knew you. He didn't, but I guess his office did... they got me your number in Columbus."

"Where is Dub's gear? Did the officers take it?"

"No, they didn't even ask about it. The nurse put his stuff in a locker, I think."

After checking with two of the floor staff, they found Dub's clothes and pack in the corner of a surgical waiting room. "We should inventory this stuff right now; I imagine that the cops will get back to it eventually."

A nurse in green scrubs approached. "Mrs. Stensvahl, Doctor says you can see Mr. Stensvahl briefly. They have decided to transport."

"Can Mr. Clay come with me?"

"I'm sorry, ma'am, doctor mentioned only you."

Clay put in: "Nurse, do you have someone that can take notes? I need to inventory his possessions with a witness present."

Nurse Lopez looked perplexed; she thought for a brief minute, then said, "I'll see if one of our volunteers can help. Now, Mrs. Stensvahl, if you will come with me..."

The volunteer turned out to be a cheery looking Hispanic woman, eager to be of help.

Clay explained what he wanted – he would unpack Dub's goods on the table and the woman, Rosie, would write each item down. John Henry thought perhaps she seemed a little dubious, but forged ahead anyway. He soon discovered that she was recording his comments in Spanish. His comb became *peine*; socks were noted as *calcetines* (5); *capillo de dientes* for tooth brush and so on. She hesitated over toothpick until he held the container up – she immediately recorded them as *picadiente*. After setting out the usual couple shirts, pants and personal gear, in the bottom of the pack he found three small, gritty cloth bags. They were a few inches in height and width with drawstring tops. He opened one and peered in. Half to himself, he said, "Ore samples?"

Rosie's eyes widened. "Oro?" she questioned. Gold?

"No oro– 'ore' – penas...piedras," he said. Rocks.

"Oh," she smiled, "rooks."

"Yeah, rocks, ore, minerals..."

"Ah! Minerales!" and she beamed at him.

Dianne Stensvahl returned as he was repacking the gear. "What would you like me to do with Dub's stuff, ma'am?"

"Well, we can't leave it here, I guess. Would you put it in my car for me, John Henry? Oh... is there anything there that you can use?"

"Maybe, ma'am – let me think on it. Maybe... he has a Katadyn water filtration system I haven't seen before – I might could use that."

"Help yourself to whatever you need."

Together with Rosie they went over the contents of his utility belt. The ubiquitous multi-tool, an old Marine Corps E-tool, canteen. *The usual*, he thought. *It's what is not here...*

"Interesting," Clay commented, "no holster, no ammunition. The shooting must have been all on the part of the bad guys."

"John Henry, when I talked to Dub – he sends you his thanks, by the way – he has just one request."

"Yes, Ma'am?"

"He doesn't want any law enforcement involved. He asked that you search by yourself, that you not talk about this to the Forest Service or to the Sheriff, or especially to the media."

"Ma'am? I have to get a permit to enter the wilderness. I have to tell them where I'm going to be and what I'm going to do. I can't just not talk to them."

"He said you'd object, but that you knew how to get it done. And, John Henry, it's my daughter that is lost or hurt up there. Please... please help us out."

"Did he have anything to say about what happened up there?"

"Only that he remembers being jumped by three men and yelling at Julie to run. The next thing he knew he was here coming out of anesthesia."

Clay thought, *that seems like an awfully long time to be out of it. Several hours...maybe he was awake part of the time and just doesn't remember...*

After a few minutes more discussion, Clay reluctantly agreed to Dub's terms. *I know I'm making a mistake,* he thought, *if I can't find her in a day or two, I can still blow the whistle, I guess. And it is her kid. It would helpful if I knew what this was really about.*

On the way out of Silver City, Clay made a stop at the post office, where he helped himself to three medium sized flat-rate mailing cartons. Carrying the three ore bags obtained from Dub's pack, he placed a heavy bag into each carton and packed the remaining space with balled-up paper from a waste container. Clay then scribbled a note thet he stuck into the lightest of the cartons. He fished in his memory for a bit, then filled out labels for each, took them to the counter and mailed them. He next went to a supermarket. In the market, he looked for canned Danish bacon, but had to settle for a two pound container of thick sliced domestic. He chose a package of the hickory smoked sugar treated variety. Clay then gassed up the truck and headed north.

The Gila

New Mexico Highway 15 runs north out of Silver City through Pinos Altos, the site of the original strike in the area and now a 'suburb' of Silver City. It then winds tortuously through the national forest toward the Gila Cliff Dwellings. Just across the imaginary line that demarks the boundary of the Gila Forest, a two-track ran up the hillside, then twisted its way back into the forest. He drove by it the first time without seeing it. After a few miles he realized his mistake, did a careful three-point turn and backtracked. He almost missed the turn a second time, the track blended easily into the duffed-over hillside. Ponderosa pine dominated the slope; orange bark plates on mature trees made them seem even bigger than they actually were. There was a scattering of pinyon and juniper but little underbrush. The two-track took him first up, then across the hillside, which he now realized was a *mountainside.* Several switchbacks further he found himself at the edge of what is generally called a park in this part of the country; this one a flattish opening in the woods with a few trees scattered through it. *About 80 by 100 meters,* he thought, with a small cabin at its head. There were about three cords of firewood neatly stacked off to the southwest side and a small pile nearby waiting to be stacked.

He could see no smoke at the chimney, but the pungent odor of a pine fire reached him even through the closed windows of the truck. A WWII Jeep stood off to the side of the track, partially covered with a dirty white tarp; a new F-150 was parked a dozen meters closer to the cabin. The clearing extended to a knob to the northeast where the terrain fell away revealing a gorgeous view out over the Gila. *Retirement,* thought John Henry, *can really be tough sometimes.*

He purposely slammed the truck door as he dismounted, started toward the cabin and shouted, "Hello the house!"

A few seconds later a figure appeared in the screen door

opening. "C'mon up and set yourself."

Chief Ranger (Retired)Y.B. Smith was a compact man of about 70, pink cheeked and clean shaven. "John Henry, how are you? Beer?" he offered. His tee-shirt was soaked in spite of the slight chill in the morning breeze. He mopped his face with a small hand towel.

"No, sir, but thanks. Gotta lot of folks to deal with yet today. Man, retirement seems to suit. Good to see you." They shook hands, then embraced as old friends.

"Yeah. When you gonna quit the rat race?"

"Y.B., I'll be able to collect Social Security in a couple of years. If I add that to my little pension and work about 600 hours a week, I ought to be able live as good as you do." Then he added, "This place is just great. It looks to really suit you. How's your health?"

"Gettin' by, John Henry, getting' by."

"You and Matty still see each other?"

"Oh, yeah, she comes up for a few days every now and again. Making sure that I don't off and die on her, she says."

"This place a part of the Forest?"

"No, I suppose that you could call this a part of Pinos Altos, but it's actually not a part of the village. When they put together the National Forest there were several tracts already in private hands. Some were bought up with a few of them leased back to the sellers, but this tract was one of the ones never included. I've had my eye on it for years, finally convinced the owners to sell to me when they went into a rest home."

They chatted for a few more minutes, when Clay broached the reason for his visit. "I know you heard about the shooting over to the Mimbres. I kind of bought into this mess, and I'm hoping you can bring me up on background."

"I got more information than I need. Bush telegraph... and I monitor the service frequencies when I'm bored; pretty good reception up here."

Clay described his brief visit and conversation with Dianne Stensvahl. "I'm going to request a back country permit to try to find the kid. I need to get up to speed on this whole thing before I go up there, though...I need to know whose toes to avoid, where the egos are. And I'll tell you honestly, Y.B – I don't think I have anything like the whole story from his ex, and I certainly have nothing from ol' Dub."

"Ah, well, let's see... early morning; trail crew on the way back to the station – they are working on 791 – hear shots around the bend up on Black Run. Like damn fools they charge the scene, couple bad guys – maybe three of them? – take off back down Gooseberry Canyon toward the Lake Road. Ah, you remember Izzy Garza? Seasonal guy, been around forever? Well it's his crew, him and three volunteer tree-huggers; they find Dub, he's been holed a couple three times. They patch him back together as best they can, drag him out to the Cienaga, call in a chopper. Had to bring the helicopter clear from El Paso. Medivac takes him to Silver. All the Feds are tied up over in the Blue, so the Acting Chief, she closes the Wilderness until the crime scene can be assessed. Meanwhile, the bad guys are gone. Nobody's figured out what's happened 'cause Mrs. Dub apparently doesn't know, and I guess ol' Dub, he ain't sayin'."

Clay nodded agreement.

"You know, old Dub's luck is still running."

"How so?"

"Well, think about it," Smith said, "hardly anybody ever goes up into the Mimbres. It is some of the loneliest and roughest country anywhere. So a few weeks ago, a trail improvement grant comes through from the Conservancy boys, or some such – just about the time they start laying off the seasonals. So we got a trail crew working for Izzy, who probably knows more than most EMTs simply because he's been around so long. And along comes Dub Stensvahl, gets himself shot, and instead of dying right there along the trail, gets saved by Izzy... most unlikely of circumstances. Go figure."

"OK, why was he in the Mimbres in the first place? He just want to take his daughter on a back country hike? Like you say, that's some tough countryside."

"Well... I donno, Clay. Dub worked in the Gila and the Mimbres both back a few years ago. I know of at least one party he guided up that way. He must know his way around some, he spent a lot of time up there... man, if you wanted to get away from the rest of the world for a while, wouldn't the Mimbres be ideal?"

"Y.B., if you wanted to gun somebody down and not have it discovered for a while…"

"That's a little hard to buy into. I mean, who's going to find him in there, let alone go marching into the mountains without any wild idea of where he is."

"I suppose the first question I should have asked: did he have a back country permit?"

"Would he have been bothered by a minor technicality like that?"

"Okay, silly question." Clay considered, then: "We know momma is scared to death her kid has been snatched by these characters, or is laying hurt up there somewhere and is going to die – or is lost and wandering and will get hurt and die. And, frankly, any of that could be right. The problem is that neither she nor Dub want to make a missing report on her. They gimme a dozen reasons they want me hunting instead of the massed forces of Uncle Sam. Their privilege, of course, but it doesn't make much sense. And now I gotta go in and sell your acting chief ranger on letting me amble up to the scene of the crime by my lonesome after she's issued a close order."

"Selling Ms. Brubaker? I wish you all the luck in the world."

"She gonna be a tough sell?"

"Ah… Wanda Brubaker has spent most of her career in law enforcement, and it shows. Some of the boys call her 'Ms. Ballbreaker.' I'd walk easy, John Henry."

Clay showed a faint smile, "I walk easy around all the women, YB."

Smith raised an eyebrow. "Lyin' sack," he said, but he smiled when he said it.

"I've been up the main trail once in my life, when I first come out here. Can you show me on a 7 ½ minute map how to get up there? Or give me directions?"

"John Henry, don't you have a GPS?"

"Well, ah, yes… but I keep it in my pack. I'm sorry, Y.B., I still like to do it the old fashioned way."

Smith shrugged, but made no comment. Walking to a small desk he picked up a piece of copy paper and a *Smithsonian Magazine*, motioning Clay to the kitchen table. He sat down and started to sketch a rough map, using the magazine for backing.

He then flipped the paper over and in a strong hand he wrote:

Dir to shooting – Lake Rd N from jct 35, go about 8 mi to Horseshoe Camp Trailhead FT 805 due E of parking lot – you can ford Ruby Creek just above Weber Creek

"You'll find a camp parking spot opposite the trail head. Don't leave anything – anything - in the vehicle. Not everyone in the woods is entirely trustworthy these days."

805 follows N side Weber Cr about 4 mi, crosses just N of fork w/Black Run. 805 then turns N, but you take FT791 going E into Gooseberry Can.

Smith paused, reread what he had written so far. Then: "Alright, Gooseberry is almost a slot at this point. Helluva scramble at two spots, last time I was up there. Stay on the track when you break out – there are a couple of cairns – until you hit the Cienaga. Notice that the spelling is 'Cienaga' with an 'a' in the middle – don't ask why."

791 follows Bl Run a mile or two, then crosses thru Cienaga, picks up S side of Black Run after a few mi.

"While that's what it's called, it's not a real cienega... more like a few acres of ribboned sand and gravel, gets flooded a bunch some years."

Shooting is just W of 791 crossing No Name Creek. This is 10-12 mi E of Ruby, Scene taped off but game tr leads around to S a few hund ft.

"No-Name may or may not be running right now... but I'd give odds there's water in it. Look for a small notch against the southeast face with ferns around it – that's where the No-Name trail takes off. The trail that you will want, though, starts at the south side of the Cienaga, sort of where Black Run ox-bows. That will keep you clear of the crime scene." He considered again, "Sounds like Dub was comin' down by that wet patch when he ran into the guys that shot him. I've heard said they're *traficantes,* but I can't for the life of me figure why drug runners would be there."

"Who else? Nobody be up there armed with AKs unless they were humping drugs... would they? Or maybe the Escalara Brothers... "

Y.B. shrugged again. "Beats hell outa me."

And, crossing both minds was, *What was Dub doing up there?*

Y.B. almost said, *Good luck getting past Miz Ballbreaker,* but he didn't.

Reserve, New Mexico

"Hey. Bro..."

"Mmmmm?"

"What's a lepton?"

"Say again?"

"The clue is, 'a lepton with no charge.'"

"You got any letters?"

"Yeah... I got blank-blank-U-T-R-blank-blank-O."

"Neutrino."

"OK, here's one... 'Lake Titicaca forms part of its border'– seven letters, third one is 'L.'"

Eddie Sam looked up briefly from the John Sandford detective story he was reading. "Try Bolivia," he said.

"How about this one: "Half-court shot, often."

"Ah... I have no idea. You oughta save that one for John Henry, he's the basketball player."

Martin faked a scowl. "Big frickin help you are." Then he considered a minute and asked, "Was he really a pro? NBA and all that?"

"Man, I guess he was. Donno about the big league, but I know he played against the Globe Trotters. Get him to tell you."

It was quiet for a few minutes longer in the Reserve motel room. Martin studied his crossword for several minutes then broke the silence again, "You hear about the big raid down in Columbus?"

Eddie slipped a marker into his book and with a stage sigh, set it aside. "No, Bro, tell me about it"

"Big cock fight, man. Sherriff arrested a bunch of guys, including a couple Columbus cops."

"No kidding? Who'd they take down?"

"Well, one of 'em was Poochie. Not much love lost between the Sherriff and Poochie."

"I hope they threw away the goddam key!" Then,

"Martin, where did you hear this?"

"They had a copy of the Deming paper tacked up at the Ranger Station when I went up there. Poochie claimed he was working undercover."

"The only undercover work he ever did was in a whore-house... anything else going on?"

"Guy got himself shot over in the Mimbres. You might have known him, name was, like, Dub or something."

"I'll be go-to-hell! That's Clay's buddy. A basketball guy. Stuck him good a couple of years ago."

"What was the deal?"

Eddie thought for a minute. Then he said, "Dub Stens-vahl. He got crossways with Old Man Escalara. A drug deal or something went bad, I guess. To keep from getting knee-capped I heard he borrowed some from his ex, then hit John Henry up for a bunch of cash. I think he knew Clay through some basketball coach. I told John Henry that he was crazy to give Dub the money, but he did it anyhow."

"I'm surprised. It ain't like John Henry just fell off the taco wagon."

"Mr. Clay said to me: 'he needed it, I had it; case closed.' Unquote."

"Then what?"

"Then, the bastard took off. Skipped out. Disappeared. Frankly, I thought he was gone forever. I wonder when he came back. Or why, come to think of it"

Ranger Ballbreaker

Back on Highway 15, headed north into the Gila National Forest, Clay had his hands full driving; the next 20 miles or so of road were a series of switchbacks and hairpins rarely allowing speeds of more that 25. It took him almost 45 minutes to reach the junction with New Mexico 35, the Lake Roberts turnoff. He swung to the right past the NMDOT storage yard and the old Gray Feathers Lodge. Doc Watson was picking *Black Mountain Rag* on the stereo. John Henry Clay was thinking bad thoughts about Dub Stensvahl. Now he had to get past Ranger Ballbreaker. "I suppose the next thing will be a letter from the IRS," he said aloud.

South of Lake Roberts he passed through a ramshackle collection of buildings the locals called Mimbres Flats. Rt. 35 straightened out for a short stretch; as he increased his speed he recognized the turnoff to the Wall Lake Road. *Well, with any luck at all, I'll be headed up there shortly,* he thought. A few miles south of the Wall Lake Road he saw the sign for the Mimbres Ranger Station, and he turned right into the dusty parking lot.

Seasonal Ranger José Ortega stuck his nose in Ranger Wanda Brubaker's office door and announced: "There's some big dude out here wants a back country permit."

"You tell him the wilderness is closed until further notice?"

"He says it is a special case; anyway, he wants to talk to you – personal, like"

"Shit. Alright, send him back." Acting Chief Ranger Wanda Brubaker was above medium height, fiftyish, and had the look of a dedicated runner. Her dark, bobbed hair was slightly askew as though she had just run her fingers through it.

Clay, battered Celtics cap in hands, ducked through

Brubaker's door and said, "Ma'am? I'm John Henry Clay."

"I am aware of who you are, Mr. Clay," she said flatly. "What can I do for you?"

He noticed that she had a copy of Hannah Nyala's *Leave No Trace* next to *The Secret Knowledge of Water* by Craig Childes, on her desk. *Yes, she is a heavy duty reader,* he thought.

"Ma'am, I was hoping that I might be able to get up into the Mimbres yet today. The man at the desk tells me that it is closed."

"Mr. Clay, we have had a serious crime committed in the Wilderness. Until a forensics team can get up there to look the situation over, the Wilderness is closed, period. Further, it is my understanding that almost all of the area's law enforcement officers are busy attending to the FBI's needs in a search in Arizona, so I don't expect anyone here any too soon."

"Ah...well, yes ma'am. That's what I wanted to talk about. I mean, that fella got himself shot here the other day. Seems there is more to the story than has been told so far."

"Mr. Clay, I am a patient woman. What is it you seem to have trouble understanding about the word 'no'?"

"Ranger Brubaker, ma'am, the man they shot? Dub Stensvahl? He was in the backcountry with his daughter. When they brought Dub out, they didn't know about the daughter. She is either still up there, hurt or lost, or maybe taken by the shooters."

"What has that got to do with you? Why hasn't this been reported?"

"Yes, ma'am. Among other things, the family doesn't want publicity if she is being held, so they don't want to make a report. And from what you tell me, it doesn't sound like you could mount much a search right now, anyway. I volunteered to help, and I'm hoping that you can understand the problems."

"I understand that in spite of the fact that you know that the wilderness is closed, you seem to think you are special. It seems to me that the reasoning for not starting a real search is very, very thin. If it were my kid lost I'd be hollering for all the help I could get.

"Why should I allow you access? Can you do what ordinarily it takes a dozen or so people with special training to do? The first thing you will do is crawl all over the crime scene looking for tracks. I can't allow that. I won't allow that. Mr. Clay, that is why I ordered the forest closed. The forensics people have not yet had a chance to go over the scene."

"Ma'am, is your protected area taped off?"

"That is the last thing the crew did before they left."

"Supposing I were to give you my word of honor that I won't go near it?"

"Mr. Clay, I understand that you mean well and that you are probably an honest man, but how do you expect to track this kid – how old is she?"

"She's 15, ma'am, and I understand that she has some woods experience. To tell the truth, ma'am, I'm scared the weather's about to change. If she's still up there..." His brow furrowed for a moment as he went on, "According to what I've been able to learn, Stensvahl was coming down a No-Name Creek trail just above Black Run when he was shot. Your trail crew was coming southwest on the main trail so we're reasonably sure that he wasn't on the trail ahead of them, and there are no other logical access points, so he must have come down No-Name. None of your folks saw the daughter, so either the bad guys got her out ahead of them, or, more likely, she's still up there either hurt or scared silly."

"Go on, Mr. Clay."

"Yes, ma'am. Y.B. Smith says there is a game trail swings south around part of the Cienaga and then angles up the hillside, meets the creek trail a couple hundred meters above your taped area. My bet is that I will pick up her trail well above Black Run and the Cienaga. If I don't, then I give it up as a bad deal – she's not there. I don't need to look over your crime scene. But I know that she is somewhere up there in the mountains close to No-Name."

Wanda Brubaker considered. If she continued to forbid access, sooner or later she was going to look like a heartless bureaucratic bitch. She'd had enough of that already. If Clay screwed it up, the onus would be on him.

"Mr. Clay, I'd like to believe you. If you give me your word you will not cross the tape – or, in fact, go anywhere near it – you can have a permit, but only to do exactly what you tell me you are going to do. You are a good enough tracker to understand that if you do violate the scene, we will know it. And, Mr. Clay? If you are not as good as your word, I will personally nail your balls to that wall right over there. Understood?"

"Yes, ma'am, Ranger Brubaker, thank you, ma'am." He caught himself just before her name came out "Ballbreaker."

Forest Trail 791

Wall Lake Road had not been graded in quite a while, he decided. Although the first few miles were in reasonable condition, it soon deteriorated to washboard, except where it was rutted from recent rains. After what seemed like an eternity of bone jarring, he found what passed for a car park together with a carved wooden sign pointing one way to the Horseshoe Camp and the other to the trailhead.

Clay checked over his pack and utility belt, then the contents of his pockets. He looked at his phone for messages. There were three; he recognized Eddie Sam's number and played the message, "Hey Big Fella, Martin and I are stuck in Reserve. Gimme a call when you get a chance." Clay turned off the phone and tossed it into the truck ashtray. *I'm in a dead zone now*, he thought, *it won't be any better up there...*

Forest Trail 805 was in pretty good shape, he noted. The climb from 7200 feet toward the Continental Divide which lay to the east started gently enough; the trail itself was wide enough most places for two to walk abreast. After a mile or so the gravelly soil gave way to a pathway composed mainly of embedded cobbles and occasional patches where the bedrock was exposed. Now the trail narrowed to little more than a game trail with cairns marking it from time to time. It followed the north side of Weber Creek for the most part with dry-foot crossings where it was necessary to shift to the south side. Clay made good time until just after crossing Weber Creek again to follow Black Run.

FT805 continued to the northeast with Weber to meet the Divide Trail, but his directions indicated that he was to now follow FT791 that eventually ended at the Kingston Overlook, some 20 miles distant. Visions of a jaunty European hiker flashed in his mind, then he thought of New Zealand's Milford Track and the few brief days there he spent as a free walker. He found himself humming *Wabash Cannonball*, and wondered if he were starting to lose it.

Leaving Weber he found a much rougher environment. While the path itself was not in bad shape, low usage had allowed brush to almost envelop it in places. *Izzy's trail crew must have decided enough was enough when they put Dub on that chopper. They sure as hell haven't done much with this end.*

Gooseberry Canyon was no treat, either. It was a narrow passageway between the Weber watershed and the higher Black Run. Where Clay entered it heading southeast it was fairly broad with the stream varying from several feet wide to places where it was barely a broad trickle over rock falls. The canyon soon narrowed to perhaps a dozen meters, at which point John Henry encountered the first scramble. A major fall had taken place years ago, blocking the creek flow partially and creating what Southwesterners call a "tank." Gradually the tank filled with debris from upstream and what little water might have been held by the tank now seeped away through the rock slide and rock/gravel fill. The rockslide remained as a barrier to two-footed traffic, necessitating a climb of some 10 feet.

Clay slipped off his pack, and selecting a stout alder sapling, cut it near ground level and stripped it of its twigs. He then took one of his tie-down ropes and attached one end to his pack, the other to his utility belt. A cairn near the south wall marked the most likely place to make an ascent. Using his free hand as well as his new staff to aid his balance, he climbed to the top despite the protests from his knees, then hauled the pack up after him. The trail, such as it was, meandered for several hundred meters beyond the tank before apparently stopping at a second fall. He covered that distance quickly, then examined the barrier, and decided that he'd need both hands and both feet for this one. He repeated the roped-pack maneuver, adding his hiking staff, and literally scrambled to the top of the 12 foot barricade. At the top, he sat down on a bathtub sized boulder to catch his breath before recovering his gear.

The afternoon was on the wane; he knew he'd have

to find a camping spot fairly soon. Ahead, he could see what appeared to be a broadening of the canyon. Alder brush and shrub willows thickened and the stream bed itself broadened considerably. At the mouth of the canyon, Black Run veered to the north but a cairn marked a trail leading out onto a bench several meters above the creek. This gradually turned to the ENE. Clay figured he'd encounter the Cienaga after about a mile and a half. *45 minutes if I'm lucky.* He also noted that if he were going to make a camp while there was still light he'd better get his ass in motion.

After just 38 minutes by the pocket watch attached by a thong to his belt loop he found himself on a bench overlooking what Y.B. Smith had called the Cienaga. It would be logical to expect this area to be boggy or swampy, *cienega* being Spanish for bog, at least a part of the year, but as Smith had promised, it seemed to be a rather broad expanse of beribboned sand and gravel. Light flows of water were present in some of the channels, others were dry but for the occasional small pond or puddle. He knew these were the result of fairly recent scattered thunder showers. When the fall rains came – make that if they came – this place would be impassable. *The Spanish hung names on everything,* he thought. *I wonder what benighted soul named this one. Or maybe some prospector...*

He selected a spot well back on the bench overlooking the Cienaga, in the shelter of a jeep sized boulder and a half dead alligator juniper. Retreating into the ponderosa pine stand on the hillside, he found a rotting deadfall. He carefully kicked loose several branch stubs and carried them back to his camp. Clay cleared an area about 6 feet in diameter and arranged rocks in it to make a fire ring about half that size. Making tinder from pine needles, twigs and bark scrapings piled against one of his pine knots, he used his lighter to start the blaze. Next he collected water from the creek in his coffee pot and set the pot to heat next to the fire. Waiting for the water to boil he found a fairly flat spot near the boulder and swept it clear of debris and rocks. That done, he examined the area for possible scorpion retreats, then collected a couple loads of pine needles, spread them out, again removing debris and cones.

Clay then retrieved the telescoping camp stool from where it was tied to his pack, extended the three legs to their 26" length placed it several feet from his fire, and with a sigh, sat down.

When the water had boiled sufficiently, he added some to a dry mac-and-cheese packet, then added Nescafe to the remaining water. Dinner was served. He thought, *At my tender age, why do I do this?*

His thoughts strayed to the other night. *She knows now,* he thought. *She's the one that has to keep career and life in separate compartments. 'Ne'er the twain shall meet'...?*

He missed the breeze; things did not feel right. Normally, light down-canyon air movement coincided with the approach of dusk but on this evening there was none. The almost overpowering silence was broken only by an occasional raven's call, otherwise there was nothing. And, he noted, a lone nighthawk wheeling after insects represented the only real wildlife activity. Clay figured he was being uneasy for no reason, decided to put it out of his mind. He had a final cup of coffee followed by his cholesterol meds, brushed his teeth and using the camp stool for support, lowered himself to the ground cloth. He unzipped the pop tent, and wormed his way into his oversized sleeping bag. Somewhere off to the southwest he heard the rumble of thunder. The last thing he remembered before dropping off to sleep, was thinking, *I'd better be careful... this is starting to play like a cheap novel...*

Ciudad Juarez

In Ciudad Juarez, over a hundred miles off to the south-east, Carlos Ramirez-Torres stepped from the car in front of his home, aided by his armed chauffer. Ramirez was a well placed manager in the offices of Credite-Suisse, but the driver was a precaution he deemed hardly necessary. At that moment, two boys aged 13 and 15, approached rapidly on skateboards. Ramirez had barely noticed them, and never even heard the shot, let alone felt the impact of the 9mm hollowpoint in his forehead. The driver got a glimpse of the older boy's face and of the gun just before he, too, died.

The two boys disappeared into the evening.

Day 2

La Llorena

Clay woke slowly. His pocket watch read 6:11; day should be beginning. Working his way out of the tent he found a dark gray world. He observed droplets on the ground cloth and on what passed for soil up here on the bench. He could see less than a few meters in the dense fog. It seemed to him that every joint in his body ached as he struggled out of his sleeping bag; he remembered all too well the days when he could pop out of a bedroll in seconds.

He sat there and spent a few seconds orienting himself, then teased the embers of last night's fire into a small blaze next to the coffee pot. Using the stool for purchase, he heaved himself to his feet, walked well up the bench to relieve himself and found his way back by the glow of the fire. He built it up with the two remaining pine knots which seemed to help dissipate the immediate fog. It was beginning to lighten somewhat but he noted that he still could not see anything beyond 8 or 10 meters.

Intellectually, he understood that the phenomenon we call fog is simply a cloud that instead of being airborne, lies on or close to the ground. He knew that fogs/clouds were the result of any one of several absolutely natural causes, and not at all uncommon at this altitude. He understood that fogs were made up of fine water droplets suspended in the air, and that sound could be amplified many times in this wet environment. This morning's dead silence and motionless air – especially after last evening – were nothing short of eerie, flying in the face of rationality. He shivered in spite of himself.

He felt the presence before he saw it. Off to the left, in the periphery of his vision, something or someone ethereal shimmered in the fog. As he turned his head slowly toward it, the mists intervened. Then as quickly as it had gone away, the figure appeared again, several feet to the right of where he last thought he had seen it. For several seconds the figure did not move, then slowly slipped back into the fog.

John Henry loosened the snap on his holster.

For several minutes the figure remained out of his sight. Just as he was beginning to think he was having visions, the figure reappeared. He could see that it was probably female, wrapped in a blanket from head down. He had heard the legends of La Llorena, the Weeping Woman, who forever lamented drowning her children, and the hair stood up on the back of his neck. His mouth went dry, and he shivered again. He needed to force himself to do something...

"Hola, Abuelita," he finally greeted, and gestured with his cup. *"Por favor,* join me by the fire with a cup of coffee." The figure shimmered, maintaining its stance. Finally, the figure noiselessly glided toward him, face shrouded by the blanket. About five meters away she (it?) stopped short and appraised him with a cold eye before approaching closer. Clay offered the coffee cup.

She took a deep swallow, glared back at him and growled with a voice from deep within, "John Henry Clay, you make the world's worst goddam coffee."

"Well, dammit, Agnes, if you don't like it, make your own. You come sneaking up here without so much as a 'hello the fire' and then you have the gall to bitch about my coffee!"

"Gave you a twitch or two, though, didn't it. Admit it." She chuckled down deep in her throat.

"You're lucky I didn't blow your ugly head off, you old bat."

"John Henry, that little pepper-pot you carry might scare lizards and snakes, but it would take more than a little birdshot to rattle these feathers."

"You might be surprised, old woman; the first load may be birdshot, but I guarantee you the second isn't. And damn sure nobody'd blame me for doing it, seeing as how it was you."

"John Henry, you are just pissed because this little old woman snuck up on the mighty tracker and scared the bejesus out of him. Phoo."

Agnes Two Pony pulled the blanket more tightly around her shoulders and squatted close to the fire. John Henry had long ago decided that he'd never be able to guess her age any closer than between 50 and 80. He'd be surprised if she weighed more that 120 pounds but she could shoulder a man-sized pack and then keep pace with anyone for days at a time. She was a genuinely good tracker although she could be as erratic as she could be committed. Agnes kept her own counsel, but could be good company when she wanted to be. She could be one of the boys, but someone you didn't dare screw around.

"OK, Agnes... where, what and why?"

"Well, Mr. Clay, seems Ms. Wanda don't trust you a whole bunch. She sent me up here to keep you out of trouble. I probably left the Ranger Station an hour after you did... I leave anything out? Oh, yeah – I run out of daylight as I was leaving Gooseberry Canyon so I put up there for the night. Between those size 13 tugboats you call shoes and your campfire, any blind idiot white man could have tracked you here."

"Size 16, thank you," he corrected her. "So, just what are your sworn duties this trip?"

"First off, keep you away from her 'crime scene' and failing that, take serious notes so that she can permanently attach a part of your anatomy to the wall. Don't mind me, I'll just watch, thank you. I'm supposed to hold the fort here until the Feebees can relieve us, the unwashed." She thought for a moment and chuckled again. "Of course, Ranger Ballbreaker didn't say anything about *me* staying out of it..."

They made a breakfast of trail bars and coffee. Agnes Two Pony commented, "You heard about your buddy? Eddie Sam? The Feds called him off the hunt, then called in the dogs."

"Yeah, he left me a message from Reserve, but he didn't say why."

"Well, I hope that somebody nails that sonuvabitch."

"Who? Eddie or Orville?" Pause... "Agnes, I don't know much about this Orville Foss character. What's he done?"

"Ah, Orville. Oh, he come up out of somewhere around Nuevo Casas Grandes with his congregation, some kind of Mormon offshoot, I guess. Involved with a bunch of under-aged 'wives.' One of 'em got knocked up, bitched to the law. That, along with some questionable fund raising practices, like extortion, got him a lot more attention than he wanted. I wouldn't think this stuff would be federal, but..." and she let it hang there.

"Lotsa Mormons in Mexico. They just about own the Casas Grandes area. Went down after the US outlawed polygamy."

"Well, Orville Foss says he is not Mormon, and I guess Salt Lake City is only too happy to agree with him. My cousin, Tommy Lucas, says Mr. Foss thinks he is Jim Bowie and Dan'l Boone reincarnated. He might be, he's pretty good in the back country. Now you know as much as I do."

"Agnes, I'll *never* know as much as you."

That Izzy Garza's trail crew was either excited or in a hurry or both was evident. While they had taped off the area surrounding where Dub had fallen, it soon became obvious to both trackers that he had been shot while descending the No-Name Creek trail at the edge of its lower portion, then had tumbled over the rather steep embankment that rose from the Cienaga and supported that part of the trail. In addition, the men who had shot him had fired from about 60 meters away, judging by the brass scattered there. The crew had probably not even noticed, as most of the tracks had been obliterated by them, probably after they had successfully seen Stensvahl loaded into the helicopter.

The No-Name trail used by Dub was little more than a game trail that worked its rocky way up the embankment in two switchbacks; from where Clay stood he could see it disappear into the rock-strewn hillside. The partially timbered side of the mountain that held the trail was steep enough, though not as steep as the bank that made up the bottom eight or ten meters. Clay retreated from the embankment to the Cienaga's south end where he found an oxbow about 10 meters in width by perhaps a hundred in length. Cut off from the main water flow it now held only a few inches. He could see quite plainly on the levy where a game trail almost touched the water, then ran upward across the hillside with an occasional switchback for several hundred meters. It looked very much as though it joined Stensvahl's trail part way up the slope. He elected to use it.

"Agnes, I'm going on up. I'll keep to that south trail until I can pick up the creek. Somewhere up there I oughta be able to pick up the kid's track."

"You need anything, Big Guy? When you figure to be back?"

"I frankly don't know. Maybe two days, could be four. After that I'm living off the land, and that's a mighty poor scratch' right now. So make it no more than four days."

Pueblo Park

About 80 miles as the crow flies to the northwest of John Henry Clay's ascent of the No-Name Creek trail, two Navajo trackers were being deposited in the Blue Wilderness of New Mexico. The pea green truck had pulled to a stop by a sign marked 'TRAILHEAD.' Martin and Eddie unloaded their gear from the bed and dropped it in the dust.

Their Forest Service driver nodded to them and said, "I'm going on to Sheep Basin. Supposed to be some law camped out there. You guys coming back here?"

"Donno, man. We got no place to stay here. The Feds said they'd be here by this afternoon, whatever that means. I suppose that we can work back to here, or go on to Blue. Either way we are going to miss an awfully lot of territory."

"22,000 acres on the New Mexico side, another 200,000 over in Arizona. Tell you what, man – don't get too far from water. There's not much around until the rains start, then there's too damn much. And just so you know... if the weather turns, won't be nobody on this road. You get caught you could go to one of the ranches at Blue, or hike back out to Reserve, but either way won't be nobody out looking for you the way this road gets."

Martin said, "Well, you're a real comfort to my old age. Thanks for the ride, anyhow."

"Yeah. Well, good luck, guys. Don't expect those radios to do you much good back in those canyons. I hope this all works out for you."

The six mile ride in from US 180, just east of Reserve, had taken the better part of an hour. They had found themselves dumped a few meters short of the Pueblo Creek crossing, opposite the Pueblo Park campground. The camp held six or eight campsites, now abandoned for the season, originally built by the Roosevelt Administration's Civilian Conservation Corps in the 1930s. While there were a couple of outhouses, the only water was in the creek, a tributary of the San Francisco River, which eventually ran into the Blue River that led to the Gila. To the south lay the Blue Wilderness, reputedly one of Aldo Leopold's favorite haunts.

Their task, as described by the FBI's Special Agent in Charge, was simply to look for any "recent activity at likely locations within the Blue." Whatever "likely locations" meant. To Eddie the only solace was that they were still collecting their daily rate plus per diem. Martin, on the other hand, seemed to relish the continued battle of wits, as he put it. Eddie wasn't sure whether the battle was with Orville Foss or with the Feds.

"Alright, do we wait for the SAC or somebody, or just move on?"

Eddie considered. "We wait, we'll catch hell for not heading out on our own. Or maybe even nobody shows up, we could wait forever. We go ahead. We got no arrangements for pickup; we'll be strictly on our own. Either way, when the weather changes – notice I said 'when,' not 'if,'– when it changes we got to be somewhere we can get out easy and in a hurry, or we end up hoist on our own petard."

"Okay, Bro, I'm game," Martin replied, thinking, *hoist on our petard? What's with that?*

At first the trail descended to the southwest rapidly, but where it began to intercept Pueblo Creek it gentled out. Eddie thought they must be about 6000 feet here... After walking about 45 minutes, they discussed boondocking directly west up Chimney Rock Canyon, then thought better of it. "Whataya think, Martin?"

"I think if, like we decided, he stays below the Rim, he'll prob'ly wanna be within 10-15 minutes of water. Assuming he's in here, of course." He raised an eyebrow in his cousin's direction.

"Best bet'll be the West Fork, then, according to the topo, I think. You wanna lead out, Bro?"

The going was fairly easy at first. They found no recent signs of human activity even though they swept out wide from the trail from time to time. They checked side canyons, climbed short ridges and followed promising game trails, all with the same result. Droplets of rain spattered down from time to time and a full blown thunder shower pelted them for about 15 minutes until they were able to find partial shelter under an old alligator juniper. When the wind came up they were rewarded with showers of dry awl-like needles in their hair and down their backs.

Three hours later found them picking their way slowly up the West Fork of the Pueblo, scattered rain showers still dancing in their faces. Against one wall of the canyon a slight overhang and a small stand of live oak offered some small protection. Martin slipped out of his pack, shook the water from his poncho, then tried to sweep the water from his hair. Eddie, his pants soaked through below his poncho, collapsed next to one of the boulders that littered this part of the canyon and broke out a water bottle. He regarded one of their tiny radios, then made a motion as if to fling it into the creek. "Useless sonuvabitch," he muttered.

"Did you ever consider, Bro, that this is a helluva way to make a livin'?" Martin asked.

"Shit, Martin," he said, "Here we are. Like, hoist on our own petard."

"Damned by orders from afar."

"And that's the way things are!"

"When you stray from the yard."

"So where's the nearest bar?"

They looked at one another, then burst out laughing. Eddie managed to choke out, "Martin, you are the craziest damn Indian I know!"

"Standin' right beside you, Jay Silverheels, standin' right beside you."

The Tank

By 11 o'clock he had gained the apparent shoulder of this particular mountain after a climb close to 800 feet, he thought. No-Name Creek wandered downward behind him, mostly a dry bed where the flow apparently continued underground. There were a couple of small tanks with little water in them, although he thought he detected an increased flow as he neared the shoulder. His knees were letting him know in no uncertain terms that he had just climbed several hundred feet.

When he picked up Dub Stensvahl's track, he came quickly to appreciate Agnes' crack about his own shoe size. *Dub must wear a 14 or 15 EEE,* he thought. Even where Dub had misstepped on his way down, there was enough impression so as to leave no doubt whose shoe it was. Shortly after he began back-tracking Dub, he encountered a second track he was sure had been left by Julie. Her tracks going back up the slope were blurred and further apart than the descending prints, as though she was trying to run on this difficult track. She left the path several times, dodging between boulders and cutting switchbacks.

He lost the trace on a stretch of exposed bedrock as he came to what appeared to be the origin of No-Name Creek. Clay scrambled the last 12 meters to bring himself level with water spurting from a notch around a rock and debris pile. Water was backed up from the cleft in the rock behind this plug. On the upstream side of the plug, a pond, or broad tank, had formed. It was too big to fit the common definition of a *tinaja,* meaning 'jug', which was what the Mexicans called a tank. Beyond it lay a rather long, fairly broad canyon which reminded him of the hanging valleys he had seen in New Zealand. The pond – at least a couple acres in size – could have passed for a small glacial cirque were it not as shallow as it appeared to be. The canyon walls varied from about 10 to 30 or so meters in height. He could see a rivulet spilling from a ledge at the rim on the right, probably from the recent rain, he supposed. Another small stream entered the canyon from a break in the northeast wall. Beyond that, the wall was pocked at various points with what appeared to be erosion caves.

He saw alligator and single-seed juniper mixed with an occasional piñon pine. A few scraggly live oak struggled to get beyond shrub size. Scattered in the rocks and in cracks in the cliff side were prickly pear and in places, what appeared to be beargrass or maybe sotol. In odd places a few yucca managed a foothold; a couple varieties of dwarf cacti appeared among the rocks. There was even a small clump of what appeared to be mountain mahogany growing beside the game trail, and groups of small trees, barren of their leaves in the early November afternoon.

The stream feeding the pond ran in a graveled, rocky bed a couple meters wide. On the north side, the bank sloped up several feet to a broad bench which appeared to extend most of the canyon length. The bench varied in depth; it was grassy for the most part and littered in places with fallen rock of varying size. On the south side, the canyon was much more abrupt; nearest him was bench similar to the north side, but after a hundred meters or so the creek bed actually ran against the wall in several places where it rose steeply to the sky. The pond itself was partially surrounded by reeds or tulles, and appeared to be fairly clear in contrast to other tanks this time of year. *There's probably a fairly good outflow most of the time. This place is absolutely gorgeous.*

What disturbed his brief admiration was the discovery of a third set of footprints. Like the others, they were somewhat blurred by rain, but easily distinguished from both Dub's and the girl's. Her tracks led back up into the canyon north bench, his were imprinted over the top of hers in several places. He wondered, *how much does that change things?*

He decided to tackle first things first. Clay selected a space well out on the bench, several hundred meters from the tank, cleared a fire ring and rimmed it with soccer ball sized rock. He popped his tent and pegged it in place but omitted the ground cloth. He then casually moved his pack and bedroll to a group of boulders several steps from his fire ring, as though he were trying to keep the gear out of the way of other preparations. He collected firewood off the trail just below the pond outlet, laid a fire and got it going, throwing in pieces of damp pine and juniper bark along with some green juniper branches. The result was a fire producing a very pungent smoke which floated away on the up-canyon breeze.

With the basics out of the way, Clay set about making a midday meal for himself. He lit his single burner stove and added a slice of bacon to his tin skillet. When this one was done, he put in another slice; now in addition to the aromatic smoke, the smell of sugar cured hickory smoked bacon was wafting along with it. While the bacon was frying, one piece at a time, he mixed up a small batch of pancakes, ready to go into the frying pan. He tended the fire, then added a strip of bacon at intervals, obviously not in a hurry to finish his meal, at odd times feeding an accumulation of bacon grease to his fire. *If the smell of this stuff doesn't bring her out*, he thought, *nothing will.*

At the same time, without appearing to do so, Clay scanned the valley sector by sector for signs of life. He had expected to be watched, but was not surprised when he detected no movement other than wildlife. *Oh, well,* he thought, *if this goes over, fine. I knew it was a long shot before I started. Sometimes the magic works, sometimes it doesn't.*

John Henry was nibbling on a strip of bacon, about to give the whole thing up as a bad deal when he realized it might be working. He caught a movement in the very tail of his peripheral vision. He rescued the last couple bacon slices, drained the excess fat, and added batter to the pan. He then set out two tins on a fairly flat rock, dropped a fork in one and a large spoon in the other as though setting a table for two.

He ate his meal in silence, waiting for something – anything – to justify the show he was putting on. He had the feeling that he was being watched as expected, then thought perhaps that was just because he did expect it. When nothing further happened by the time Clay finished his meal, he cleaned up his dishes and set about making the camp more comfortable. *So much for the old bacon trick.*

He spent the next couple of hours scouting the valley, noting that there were three distinct sets of human tracks, easily distinguished from one another. Dub and his daughter had built a fire ring on the bench slightly to the east of where John Henry had built his. Their tracks led about the canyon in random patterns, although he could see where Dub had taken advantage of centuries-old steps carved into the rock to climb out to the northeast several times. He could see that a third set of tracks, the ones that disturbed him, seemed to have been made before the Stensvahls arrived, and at least one set were overlayed on Julie's recent tracks. He noted also that Julie showed signs of recent activity moving to and from a partial chimney in the wall several hundred meters from where he camped. Clay might have missed the mystery tracks altogether had he not been looking for them; the man seemed to be very careful of where he walked.

Campfire

Back in his camp John Henry casually moved his gear about as he seemed bent on rearranging things to suit himself. In the course of several minutes, he moved his bedroll to get much closer to the actual wall of the canyon. It was done casually; he seemed to take no notice of it.

Clay rolled rice and beans into a cold tortilla for supper and prepared to wash it down with instant coffee. He thought he saw movement off to his right as he retrieved his old Hohner Marine Band harmonica from his pack, so he settled his stool next to a boulder, leaned back and doodled his way through *Old Folks at Home*, then fooled with *Shenandoah* for several minutes. He was just starting to work his way into the *Gerryowen* when she appeared.

She stood at the edge of the bench and looked at him indecisively. Apparently making up her mind, she took a step forward and said, "Aren't you going to invite me in?"

"Well... proper protocol would seem to be for you to shout, 'Hello the fire,' or something like that before you get close enough to throw rocks," he said with a smile.

"Alright, hello the damn fire!"

"Hello yourself, come on in and set a spell. Coffee?"

She nodded, so he poured her a cup of the instant. "I hope you like it black," he said, "'cause that's what we've got."

She took the coffee, watching him closely. She was clearly tightly strung, as though she were putting up a brave front against the strong possibility of bolting at the slightest wrong move on his part. "Do I know you?" she asked

"You must be Miss Julie," he said conversationally, "I'm John Henry Clay. Kind of a friend of your mother and daddy." Clay lifted his cup in a mock salute.

He thought she was going to tear up at the mention of "daddy", but she held it in. "Is he alive?" she asked.

"He was when I left Silver. They were going to transport

him to Albuquerque yesterday, I think. I talked to your mom at the hospital, but I don't know much else."

"How do you know mom and Dub?"

"I know your daddy from basketball camps and such. I know your mom because I know your daddy."

"Like, you just happened to be passing by 'n thought you'd stay the night?"

"Like, your momma is scared to death you've been kidnapped and/or killed. She asked me to wander up here to see if I could find you. Looks like you found me. Are you alright?"

"Why'd she call you instead on somebody else?"

More a demand than question, he thought. "Well, Miss Julie, I suppose it's because what I do is track people...you know, lost hikers, little kids, young ladies in distress..."

"Is that what I am? A young lady in distress?"

"Well, ma'am, I don't know. I just met you, and you seem to pretty much in control of your situation. Are you in distress?"

"Is anyone else with you? Are you alone?"

"Yes, ma'am. Just me. What you see is what you get. Seriously, are you alright?"

She ignored him still, sipping the coffee steadily, poised as if prepared for flight, and continued to eye him distrustfully. John Henry looked her over carefully. She had her mother's build with long legs and long, expressive hands, nails bitten to the quick. He'd not expected her to have her father's fair Scandinavian hair, but there it was, plaited into a single braid down her back. Julie was attractive in a fresh scrubbed sort of way, but maybe not what you'd call beautiful, he thought. Yes, he thought, she's long but not what some would call willowy. She was wearing sweats and a tee-shirt with a light jacket tied by its arms around her waist. Clay couldn't help but notice that she was not wearing a bra. Prominently not wearing a bra. She watched him carefully for a moment then without warning, her eyes flashed, "You old pervert- HERE- YOU WANT A GOOD LOOK?"

With that she flipped the hem of her shirt up to her eye-level fully exposing her chest. Clay shook is head sadly. "Ma'am, you seen two, you seen 'em all," he said quietly, adding a piece of wood to the fire.

Her eyes brimmed with tears, but she didn't move.

"I'm sorry, Miss Julie, I didn't mean to give offense." He considered what to say next. "Your momma asked me to look in on you, see if you were alright. Are you?" he asked again.

She was still belligerent. "You think so? Like, I'm sitting up here at the end of the universe not knowing, what the hell happened or what's going to happen. My old man's been shot down and carted away. Like, I am almost out of food. It's starting to get cold at night. I am so goddam strung out that I... goddam it!" and she couldn't finish but broke out in sobs.

Well, he thought, *I guess the manual doesn't cover this...*

She squatted with her back against a rock facing the fire, as though the outburst never happened. Clay toyed with the harmonica, rendering *Wabash Cannonball* and working his way through a couple of Woody Guthrie's. He was working on Leadbelly's *Goodnight Irene* when she broke into his thoughts. "I need to go back home, don't I?"

"Prob'ly it'd be a good option."

"Everything is so screwed up!"

"How so?"

"It just is."

He considered. "OK," he said finally.

He went back to *Goodnight Irene,* improvising a couple of bars that on reflection, he didn't much care for. He slipped the harp into his pocket and looked over at her for a moment. She didn't meet his eye.

"How'd you get to be a tracker?"

"Used to fool with tracking when I was a kid. It was fun to see who made what track, see if I could follow for any distance. Worked one summer in the Bradshaws, in north Arizona, for an old rancher; he taught me more. Fought a couple of wars in Central America beside native trackers, learned a lot. In the jungle as well as the desert. Now I get called out once in a while by the Park Service or sometimes the forest boys to help them out. A little extra beer money."

"What do you... I mean, like, how do you track people... or anything, for that matter?"

"Mostly it's what they call situational awareness. You heard of that?"

"Go on."

"I guess it is all about learning to see, learning to observe. You gotta know who or what you are tracking. What kind of print they leave, where they like to walk, how they walk, stuff like that. You have to understand their habits, their thinking. A deer doesn't think like a bear; a bear track doesn't look like a rabbit track. You have to ask yourself, 'what would Julie Stensvahl do in this situation?' and be ready with the answer. What you don't know, you have to intuit. And thirty years experience doesn't hurt." *OK*, he thought, *so I fudged the experience part a little.*

He could tell that she stayed with him for a few sentences, after that her mind seemed to drift.

"You hungry?"

She grimaced. "Food doesn't appeal right now."

He sensed that she wanted to tell him something, but he didn't know how to reach her. He had not been at a loss for the proper words or action very many times in his life, but this was certainly one of them. *Keep her talking. Maybe something will spill.*

"Your mom wants to know that you are alright. If you go back with me, you can tell her yourself."

"God, I'd rather do anything else."

"You sure you don't want something to eat?"

"Like, what have you got?"

"I had Mexican rice and beans in a tortilla for supper." He gestured toward his open backpack.

"Oh yuccch. You got any peanut butter? And crackers?"

"I just might be able to scrounge some up." He rummaged in his food box, produced a couple packets of PB, and found some soda crackers to go with them.

She tried to eat delicately, but peanut butter does not lend itself to that practice easily. When she was through, Julie licked the blade of her Leatherman clean, followed by two fingers that had received a light coating. She then washed her meal down with more coffee.

A long pause ensued.

"You were a basketball player. Dub's talked about you. Like, you played in the pros or something."

"Or something."

"Who'd you play for?"

He smiled ruefully. "How about the *Washington Generals*? Some folks consider them pros."

"Who were – are – they?"

"The Generals tour with the *Globetrotters*."

"Oh." Then, "Who else? Anybody I've heard of?"

"ABA. The old American Basketball Association I mean, you probably never heard of it. Club ball in Europe... a season on the Celt's taxi squad."

She looked carefully at him, then said, "You've been to some of my games. I knew I'd seen you somewhere."

"Yes, ma'am"

"What did you think? About how I play, I mean."

"Ah...well, you're OK."

"What's that supposed to mean? OK.?"

"You didn't come up here for a coaching clinic, and I didn't come up here to give one."

"No, I'm serious. I want to know what you thought when you saw my games."

"Well... ah... You are OK for someone at your level of play. You can't use your left hand, but that will come if you are serious about the game. And... you might even learn to play a little defense someday."

"I play defense now!"

"Miss Julie, you are a sucker for a ball fake, you drop your left foot... you can't cover on a give-and-go...you are slow to block out... I could go on, but like I said, this is no place for a clinic." If her ego was bruised by this exchange, she gave no sign of it.

He was surprised to note that the sun was behind the mountain, dusk was well along. They had been talking – sort of – for well over an hour he supposed.

She had assumed a serious face. "You know all about the game?"

"Ma'am, nobody knows all about the game, least of all, me." *Shift the conversation,* he thought. "Umm... seems to me you stay up here, you're going to miss some basketball practice, aren't you?"

That opened the flood gates. She flung down the empty cup and fled back up the canyon. He watched her go.

By seven the sun had disappeared behind the ridge and darkness was beginning to take the canyon. The warmth of the afternoon was replaced by a light, chill breeze so he punched up the fire and moved in closer. *Going to be a long night. Why did that set her off? I wonder if I've lost her?*

When the light was gone and the moon not yet up, Clay surreptitiously moved his sleeping gear to the canyon wall protected by a slight overhead protrusion, leaving the tent where it was. He had let the fire die down to embers and for a while went back to the harmonica, moaning out blues sounds before making his bed. Nothing stirred except for a few bats.

Somewhere a long way off, he thought maybe he heard a wolf howl.

Rolling his jacket for a pillow, he thought of Columbus, and of the other evening's activities. He pulled the sleeping bag up around his shoulders, rolled to his left and touched the little revolver resting next to his stool. The last thing to filter through his thoughts of before drifting off was Julie Stensvahl's bare breasts.

Las Chepas

A little earlier that evening, about a kilometer south and west of the tiny Mexican settlement of Las Chepas, just across the international boundary with the United States and perhaps 80 miles from John Henry Clay, two boys, one nine and the other seven, were doing what boys do, that is, fooling around. They happened to be fooling around playing *Mojados y Migras* in an arroyo they had not visited for a few days, and were completely unprepared for their discovery.

As they charged around a bend in the wash, their game of Wetbacks and Border Patrol came to abrupt end. They were brought up short by the sight of a disembodied head in more or less the center of the arroyo. At first, they did not recognize it for what it was, but as the nine-year-old approached it cautiously, he realized that he was staring at apparently all that was left of a *Grupo Beta* officer he had seen many times in the village.

When the two of them burst into the *jacal* they called home, their father shushed them, and made them tell their story from the beginning. When the boys had calmed enough to comply, he heard them out. As any good Mexican citizen and father might, he then admonished them sternly to (A) not go near the arroyo again, and (B) to keep their mouths firmly sealed shut.

Day 3

The Basketball Player

He woke several times during the night, and actually got up once to pee and stroll the perimeter of his camp. He found nothing amiss so went back to bed, but he still had concerns about the third set of tracks. *The Third Man,* he thought.

When he arose it was light but the sun had not crossed into the valley yet. He wandered casually down to the creek, then did a thorough examination of the canyon for some hundred meters around the camp. Nothing.

Clay prepared for breakfast by rehydrating some onion and green pepper flakes, then mixing them into powdered eggs. He had saved back two strips of bacon that he crumbled into the mix. Setting that aside, he sautéed a few fresh mushrooms, and when they were ready he poured the egg mixture into the frying pan and edged it into the embers of his fire. *The air has an unsettled feel to it. It will rain before the morning's out,* he thought. *I wonder where our wandering girl is today?*

He again explored the valley carefully. Of the several depressions in the north wall, four or five might be big enough to offer shelter to a couple – maybe more – people. He knew the Gila and surrounds were shot full of pit houses and pueblo-like dwellings used centuries before by the Mogollon peoples and others. It was almost impossible to explore the country for a day without coming up with some evidence of earlier inhabitants, he had discovered. On back country tours when he was able, he liked to bring touring little blue-haired ladies within walking distance and allow them to 'discover' a pueblo.

She is in one of those holes. Probably the one nearest that chimney, where it's partially screened by that bunch of junipers. Well, let her be. If she is going to come out, she will, not much I can do now.

He dumped the skillet contents into a tortilla, sprinkled it liberally with green Tabasco, and settled back on his stool. *Life ain't easy for a boy named Sue.* He decided he'd give Julie the rest of the day... maybe tomorrow, too... though he'd bet dollars to donuts they were about to get a cold front down their necks. This time of year they were no fun, either.

He thought about the other evening, just before the phone call. *Seems like so long ago.* She was an interesting woman; a fairly deep thinker; absolutely joyful in bed; and she didn't seem to mind his mustache, or at least didn't comment on it. He knew she was a reader. They had met in a used book store in Deming, ended up having coffee and spending the balance of the day together. They had 'dated' a couple of times, then, the other evening he'd made dinner for her and she'd brought a bottle of a nice cabernet. He should have called her to let her know what was going on. *Oh, well...water over the dam, now.*

Julie showed up just before lunch, wearing a bra and sweatshirt, he noted. Judging by today, nothing out of the way had happened, they were apparently still buddies. Clay invited her to stay for lunch and offered a cup of coffee, which she took eagerly. He opened a small tin of Danish ham, sliced about half of it and browned it in the skillet, sliced an onion then assembled the ingredients together with a little mustard on tortillas for them both. A handful of raisins finished off the meal.

They both sat close to the fire, waiting for the conversational ice to break. Though John Henry was used to keeping his own counsel for hours at a time, this long lull in communication made him very uncomfortable. *This is silly. I'm sitting here with a 15 year old kid and I don't know what to say.*

It was Julie who broke the barrier. "Mr. Clay, you said you met Dub at basketball camps."

"Ah... yeah, in Europe the first time, I think. Early '80s. I was playing club ball and your daddy was a Minnesota hotshot. Coach Billy Nightingale brought him over for a 'good will' camp for a bunch of Spanish kids. I was invited because I could speak Spanish, mostly."

"Where did you learn Spanish?"

"The Army sent me to language school at the Presidio, in California. I had a Mexican nanny as a little kid, so I already spoke some, and I could type so the Army figured I'd be a natural. What happened out there on the trail? The shooting, I mean?"

She looked away from him, up the valley. With a brief expression of anguish, she said, "I don't really know. We were coming down the trail... I was quite a ways behind him, when he shouted at me to get out of there and then guns went off. I ran back up the hill."

"Did you actually see him get shot?"

She hesitated, then said, "I looked back once and saw him fall. It didn't occur to me at time that he'd been shot. By the time I got to where I see what was going on, the guys with the guns were gone and four new guys were bringing Dub out to the Cienaga. I watched a while 'til a chopper came in. By then it was too late for me to do anything – I was, like, in shock or something."

"What happened to his gun? The Forest Service crew didn't find one... did you pick it up?"

"No, honest to God, I never went back down that trail. I came back here and hid."

"Mmmm... why did the two of you come up here?"

"You ask a helluva lotta questions, mister."

"Yeah, well... see, this is awkward for me, Julie, and I'm sure it is for you, too. I'm trying to understand the situation, you know? And I don't know how to go about it any other way."

She thought about that. He was pretty sure that she wanted to trust him but maybe he hadn't done anything so far to earn her trust. *Life ain't easy...*

"Julie, tell you what – can we start over? I'm just a guy doing a job. I promised your mom I'd try to find you and make sure that you are alright. So I found you, or maybe you found me… but as near as I can tell, there's some stuff wrong here that's making you very unhappy. I know you think I'm a lecherous old man – and I may be – but believe me when I tell you that the only reason I hiked up into these damn mountains is 'cause I told your momma I would."

She seemed to take his words into consideration. "How much is she paying you?" she demanded.

"I haven't asked a thing from her."

Julie took her time digesting this. Clay fished out his harmonica, wailed a train whistle, then softly played *Wildwood Flower.*

The morning's brightness seemed to go out of her; she visibly sagged where she sat.

She looked at him squarely and said, matter-of-factly, "I'm pregnant."

He must have looked baffled, because then she continued, "I'm knocked up – I'm going to have a kid. That kind of shoots basketball in the ass, doesn't it?"

"How do you know?" He regretted it as soon as the words were out.

She looked at him disdainfully. "Dumb ass question. A girl knows. I'm like two weeks late."

"You are only – what – 15?"

"Like, you think kids don't have sex just because they're kids?"

"Well no, but…"

"But what? We screwed, he didn't use protection. I'm knocked up. What do I have to explain?"

He was about to comment, then remembered that he had only been 14 when Gloria, the girl across the street, had gotten him into a wrestling match that ended up under the neighbor's bushes.

"No explanation necessary."

"So everything's changed. Basketball. School. My whole damn life."

"So everything's all over because you are pregnant? Isn't that a little drastic?"

"How the hell would you know? You never got pregnant. My life is basketball and…" She couldn't finish.

He regarded her in silence for several minutes. "Wilma Rudolph didn't think it ended her life."

"Wilma who?"

"Wilma Rudolph. They called her the world's fastest female. Back when I was growing up, she had a helluva career as a sprinter – I think at Tennessee – and she won three Olympic golds. Built a life around her family and coaching and public service. Quite a woman."

"So what?"

"Well, she did it all after she had a kid at eighteen, 'out of wedlock' as they say. She took a year off, then went back to the track stronger than ever. Never looked back, just went on with life."

She considered this, but looked doubtful.

Keeping Julie engaged was proving to be a problem from time to time. Clay had found the he could usually keep people talking for hour, even if it were only about themselves, but she was proving reticent. *OK, Julie, let's talk some more about you.*

"How long your mom and dad been apart, Julie?"

"I never knew them when they were together."

"He's been around quite a bit recently, though, hasn't he?"

"Yeah."

"Has he spent a lot of time with you? Your mom said you played ball together."

"Yeah. Like, the last couple months we'd go over to the college gym and get into pickup games. Sometimes we'd like do it every day. It was a lot of fun."

"Your daddy was a fine ball player in his time. He could take a guy six inches taller than him into the post, then make him look silly with a wicked reverse layup or something. Stuff like that."

"Dub can pass, too," she said. "He'll move between high and low posts when he's playing with smaller guys, and feed the drivers all day. He is fun to watch and he's fun to play with." She paused, then looked back at Clay and said, "It was like he was showing off for me by doing all that stuff besides scoring."

"He could score when he wanted to. And he could

defend, if he was challenged enough. I watched him play James Worthy to a standstill one night. He seemed like he had half a step on Worthy all night. Wouldn't let him work his way into the post let alone get set there. He'd stuff ol' 'Big Game James', kept him blocked off the boards. It was a real clinic, I'll tell you. Pat Reilly was going nuts on the bench."

"Mr. Clay, you said you toured with the Globe Trotters. I thought they were all black guys."

"They were. I played for the team that toured with them, the Washington Generals. Our job was mostly to lose. We did that pretty well. It was a lot of fun, but it was never real competitive basketball. Curley Neal was the Trotters captain, but the real draw was Meadowlark Lemon."

"I never heard of either of them."

"Was your dad working? Your mom said he'd only been back in Silver for a couple of months. What was he doing?"

"I don't know; he didn't say. Why all these questions about Dub?"

Clay tried to look as serious as he could. "Julie, I'm trying to figure all this out. Why we couldn't call the authorities to search for you, why Dub was apparently ambushed and shot in the middle of a National Wilderness, why it was important to bring you in here with him. I'm sorry, none of this adds up."

"Well, I guess you'll just have to ask Dub."

They spent part of the afternoon talking about the need to get themselves out of the backcountry before they were trapped by weather. Toward three o'clock, the overcast produced an occasional misting rain, with the promise of more serious stuff to follow.

They took shelter under the overhang. She looked at John Henry's bedroll, then at his tent out on the bench, but didn't say anything. She asked him about his connection with the Celtics. "That was back in '75-'76. I ended up in Boston taking a couple of courses at B.C. The taxi squad would scrimmage with both first and second teams when they were not on the road. We'd role-play, like I'd be somebody like Rambis one week or Bob McAdoo of the Knicks the next – that kind of thing."

She wanted to talk basketball. Whatever else might have been on her mind, it was obvious where her heart was. "Who was the best you ever played against?"

He took a moment to consider. "Remember, I never actually played in the NBA, and not much in the ABA. In all the time I played ball, though, there's no doubt that the toughest job I ever had was guarding Moses Malone. He was 6'10" and about 260 or so then. It was a charity game and he was just fooling around, I think, but he took me to school."

"OK, who was the best you ever saw play?"

"Best at what? Best all 'round had to be Byrd. Bar none. He was the guy you wanted to have the ball when you were down three with seconds to go. He had all the instincts. The man was pure great."

"How about Michael?"

"Gotta give Jordan his due. One helluva competitor, and both he and Larry Byrd made everyone around them better ballplayers. Hard to choose, I guess. I'd still go with Byrd in the clutch." Memories flooded back. "Guys with the Celts that I knew were all damn good. Jo-Jo White, Dave Cowans, Paul Silas... Took the league championship in '76; Tom Heinsohn was coaching then. Oh, somebody else I had to guard a couple of times in Europe was Kurt Rambis. He was an incredible rebounder."

"I've never heard of those guys," she said.

"Fame is always fleeting. You can quote me on that."

She didn't seem inclined to leave the bench. Clay toyed with his mouth organ, then said, "Can we plan to get out of here tomorrow? There is a cold front due through that will make things very bad for us if we don't." He felt safe using "we," now that they had seemingly established some sort of rapport. *Does she know about the 'third man'? I wonder. If I tell her will it sound like a bullshit attempt to scare her into leaving?*

He decided not to. The rain had picked up, then suddenly quit.

She took her time. Finally, she said, "OK, I guess. There's really nothing for me here."

"I'll be moving at zero-dark-thirty. Be down here

sometime after first light and we'll try to beat the cold." As sort of an afterthought, he said, "Julie, I am really going to have to move in the morning. I want you along, but if you decide against going..." He let the sentence hang there. It started to rain hard, again.

The Blue

By mid afternoon both Navajos were wet again and dead tired. Martin was cutting trail, working his way toward a ridgeline and having to climb one of the most difficult paths they had yet encountered. Not wanting to disturb any traces that might remain on the trail, he was skirting it as close as the terrain permitted, which, he admitted to himself, wasn't very damn close. Eddie was several hundred meters behind him, trying to decipher what appeared to be man-tracks on the old game trail.

Martin suddenly encountered an unexpected side trail leading back to the north and toward a major rock fall. On a whim, he decided to investigate this new trail. The trail rose through the juniper/pine stand, but before it got to the rock fall, it veered to the right, directly at a juniper tangle.

"Eddie?"

"Ten-four."

"Eddie, I think you better come up here. You ain't gonna like this."

Las Cruces NM

L as Cruces is a bustling, growing city. One magazine
boasted of it as the best place in the country to retire.
Pablo (Paul) Ramirez studied again the article in the *Las Cru-*
ces Sun. The story described another shooting in Juarez and
a couple of the names caught his eye. Twenty-eight guests at a
wedding in the city's west side had been rounded up and herded
into a storage shed adjacent to the church. Apparently angered
because they did not find a particular individual among the
guests, the gunmen riddled all in sight, then poured gasoline
over the bodies and set fire to them. The only one to escape
the carnage was the nine year old ring-bearer. The story did
not mention how he made his escape. The groom was one Eloy
Malachea. The best man's name, Pablo knew, was Frederico
Ramirez.

Pablo immediately dialed his cousin in El Paso. "I'm
outa here, dude. I'm gone. They nailed Fredo; you and me'll
be next." With that, he threw some clothing and personal ef-
fects into a duffle bag, slipped out the back door and into his
new Chevy pickup, parked at the curb. As he started out into
the street, a Suburban pulled alongside, and with two assault
rifles blazing, cut Pablo and the Chevy to ribbons.

Day 4

Alan Ladd

She was late. While he had expected her to be late in starting, he didn't really expect that she would be a no-show. He could go look for her, but decided against it, she could be anywhere. Maybe if he took his time on the trail... Reluctantly, he shrugged into his pack, picked up his stick and turned onto the vague game trail leading downstream. If he was to get out before night set in he had to leave now. At least the wind was at his back.

The rain of yesterday had turned to sleet in the evening hours, then to huge flakes of snow. Toward nightfall it began to snow in earnest. The wind had picked up again, driving out of the west and temperatures had plummeted. Where No-Name Creek had wandered placidly, a raging torrent had replaced it running bank-full into the now turbulent cirque. The water was now a mini-maelstrom, churning gray and white among and over rocks that had water barely touching them 36 hours ago. *If I have to wade this,* he thought, *I'm in trouble. There must better than a meter of water in the shallows.* Snow was already a few inches deep except where the rocks had blown clear or warmer soil had melted it. What little trail he could see was beginning to fill in. Earlier, a few bright blue patches had appeared in the overcast, but it had reverted to a solid deep gray, that cast little shadow detail, making the trail even more difficult in the brushy bottoms.

Worse, some stretches of trail were catching splash from the stream, making travel a business of placing each foot carefully before the next step could be taken. Where the path wandered away from the creek, it angled upward on the steepest part of the slope without actually cresting the bench between him and the cliff face. By now his poncho, while cutting a major portion of the wind, had allowed meltwater to run in rivulets, soaking his pants from the knees down.

On the west end of the pond, where earlier the small waterfall had barely trickled into the arroyo, the fall now spewed foam outward despite the fact that even more debris had gathered at the cirque's outlet. The din created by the waterfall and the surging creek combined to make a disturbing roar in the usually quiet canyon. He paused about a dozen meters from the fall to pull his hoodie down snugly around the battered Celtics cap. He turned, half facing the pond, when from back up the trail a flash of red caught his eye. She was moving rapidly – too rapidly – after him. Although she was using a stick, she slipped a couple of times as she made her way downstream.

Even as the words *Be careful* formed on his lips, she went down on her right knee, her left foot slipped out from under her, and then it was only momentum that carried her sliding down the short incline into the torrent.

Sweet Jesus, he breathed as he started back toward her, shucking his pack as he went. Her slide had been brought to a halt by a pair of partially submerged boulders, leaving her half in and half out of the water. The new blockage in the stream created by her body and pack soaked her through instantly; at the same time it served to further jam her into the rocks. He didn't hear her call out, although later he thought that she must have. Her thrashing produced nothing except the ingestion of great gulps of sandy water.

Using his walking stick to steady himself, John Henry had taken a step toward her from the trail when his own footing gave way. He found himself sitting against a small stump with one leg partly in the stream. His stick had been swept away, but he was able to reach Julie's pack by stretching with his left arm. He quickly discovered that neither of them could move – she was struggling against the water, and he could not find enough purchase from his position to help her... Or even, he mused momentarily, to get out himself and the water level was still on the rise.

Later, he couldn't say how long they worked at cross purposes to free themselves. Whether it was just seconds or several minutes, they were both damned cold and losing strength, he could tell. He found himself shouting, "Stop it... stop it! Relax! I can't help you this way!"

"I can't!" she sobbed, "I can't!"

"Dig in your heels! Push to the bank side."

"G-Godammit, I'm trying!"

At that moment, he heard from above and behind him, someone shout: "Grab on, amigo!"

The voice didn't register at first, but then rolling onto his right elbow he looked up... and into the barrel of a rifle.

When he later thought about it, he realized that two un-related and unimportant things registered in his mind during that first second or two. The first was that he was looking into the bore of a Winchester saddle ring carbine; and second, it was being extended by Alan Ladd. Grasping it by the stock, he extended it to Clay, who, by arching back grabbed it with his right hand while clinging to Julie's pack strap with his left. Between the two of them they managed to haul the sputtering and cursing girl to what was left of the path. As they stood her up, she screamed in pain, her right leg collapsing under her.

The newcomer, a small man dressed in dirty buckskins, said, in flat voice, "She's rolled an ankle."

"Or hypered her knee."

"It's my ankle! Will you dumb bastards help me?" she cried plaintively.

Alan Ladd looked at Clay, shrugged, pulled her arm over his shoulder and the two of them half dragged, half car-ried her up onto the bench. John Henry decided that the little man didn't much look like Alan Ladd, after all.

"Over there," he said, pointing to the canyon wall. They moved slowly across the bench in the indicated direction. About half way there, a distance of perhaps 10 or 12 meters, they paused, Julie muttering imprecations. The man looked over at Clay and said, "She has a mouth on her, don't she."

John Henry shook his head slowly. "Yessir, she surely

does."

With an eyebrow raised at Clay, the man started again for an apparent break in the cliff wall. "We're here," he said as the three of them reached the break. "Lemme take a look first."

Eons ago, the creek had undercut the sandstone cliff face to the point where a portion of the overhang, about 20 meters long, had fallen onto the bench below creating a hollow behind it. The light was dim, but showed the resulting cave was about 6 meters deep at its deepest and tapered from end to end. The huge rockfall itself had cracked in two places, one of them wide enough for a person to slip into the cave. Ancient peoples had divided the northwest corner into several small rooms – *very small rooms*, Clay thought as he stepped into the space behind the girl and Alan Ladd. The cave was about five meters at its high point, he thought. The cave had apparently been used heavily for shelter at one time, judging by the accumulation of soot on the roof, although there appeared to be close to a meter of clearance between the fall and the roof of the overhang. At the west end, the smallest of the rooms, probably granaries, were formed by walls about shoulder height. Two larger spaces were closer to them – maybe 3 meters or so by a couple of meters, one wall in the near room blackened by repeated fires.

Alan Ladd stopped short of this room and unceremoniously unburdened himself of Julie Stensvahl. The move startled Clay momentarily and he too, released her. She fell in a rather inglorious heap and cursed them roundly. Clay thought, *I've got to stop thinking of him as Alan Ladd,* but down deep he knew the damage was done; he'd never be able to picture the buckskin clad man again without seeing the long-ago movie star.

The man produced some lint from his fanny pack. "Sir, see if you can scrounge up some kindling. I'll fetch a couple pine knots. I'd set up right over there," he said, indicating the northwest corner of the near room. "Was I you, I believe I'd see her stripped down... and you'd ought to get into dry trousers. It'll get right cold here before the night's out."

"I'll be d-d-dammed," Julie sputtered through chattering teeth. "I won't strip with either of you s-s-sons-a-bitches
standing here!"

"Your choice," the man said, turned on his heel and
walked out of their new-found shelter.

John Henry took a reasonable tone. "Julie, you will die
here if you don't get into dry clothes and warm up. I've some
long johns in my pack. I'll get them as soon as I get a fire going." By now she was not only chattering but shaking visibly.

After retrieving his pack, Clay rummaged through the
contents and produced a pair of insulated underwear, and his
old NMU orange sweatshirt. He tossed them to Julie. She had
removed her boots, although not without some difficulty, and
started on her jeans. She looked up at John Henry.

"T-t-turn your back, you old fart. Th-th-this isn't a thrill
show!"

He did as she commanded, picked up a his change of
clothes, peeled his khakis and shorts, and stepped into dry
underwear and pants. This done, he unrolled his sleeping bag
and threw it around her shoulders while she finished redress-
ing. Next, he soaked a dirty tee-shirt in melting snow water
and wrapped her ankle in it. He spread the wet clothing on the
ruined interior walls of the pueblo. Where he was able to, he
strung some tie-down rope as a clothesline. "You don't want to
wear jeans up in this country," he commented. "They're cotton
and take forever to dry out." He wrung out her sleeping bag as
best he could, rolling it out on the main cave floor. *There's a
hopeless exercise,* he thought.

Their new found friend had returned with an armload of
pine knots and added to the fire. While the wind howled outside,
their cave furnished them not only protection, but conserved a fair
amount of the heat produced by the blaze. *That didn't take any
time at all,* Clay thought. *I'll bet he knows this canyon like the back
of his hand.* He studied the man squatting near the fire. Not quite
medium height, on the slender side of stocky. Dark blond hair,
showing some gray. Maybe in his 50's but in good physical shape.
His teeth were not good. He crouched several feet from the fire,
and clung to his rifle, the muzzle never far from John Henry.

"You come along at a good time," Clay said.

"Been watchin' you and the girl both." Pause, then: "Couldn't figure what you two was up to." Pause. "Can't figure what *any* of you people is up to. This world is just plain gone loco." He looked up at Clay, "You're sure a long 'un"

"Yessir," John Henry replied. "I come up here to fetch her out."

"You getting' paid for it?"

"No sir."

"Pure Christian charity, then?"

"No, sir. Her daddy owes me money, and her momma asked me to do it."

Alan Ladd digested this. "Like you protectin' an investment?"

"Something like that."

For several minutes, the silence was broken only by the snapping of the pine wood and the chattering of Julie's teeth. Clay unstrapped his stool from his pack, extended the legs and sat. "Save the knees," he said. "They're about shot. Can't much get down any more." He decided to take the bull by the horns. "My name's John Henry Clay... and that is Miss Julie Stensvahl. You been in this country long?"

He was ignored. "Fix her something hot to drink. That'll help."

Clay knew he didn't have anything but coffee. Hoping for something more substantial he went through Julie's pack. Inside a large zip-lock bag he found, among other things, a small diary, four tampons, two Pez containers (one empty), a cell phone, several tea bags, and there, on the bottom, three packets of a powdered cocoa drink. He heated water in silence.

After several minutes, the man offered, "Been in the Mimbres awhile...and up here, well, maybe a week or so. More excitement than I need. Lot of folks I'd just as soon not run into. I swear, I'm not too delighted to make *your* acquaintance, either."

"I'd guess that if a man wanted to be left alone, here'd be a pretty good place."

"That's the truth. Seems like I no more than settled in here than all sorts of folks started to run around. I'd be grateful, sir, if when you report to others, you could overlook my presence."

Clay nodded, then said, "I'll bet you saw the shooting."

The man smiled slightly. "You could say that. Crazy bastard cut down on a couple of guys coming up the trail, they shot back. She (indicating Julie) went a'scurryin' back up here like her butt was on fire."

"Her daddy started the fuss? We heard different."

"Mr. Clay, I don't know what you heard, or who from, but I know what I know."

John Henry frowned. Heat from the fire was starting to penetrate. Water simmering in the can, he added the cocoa mix, lifted the can off the fire with his Leatherman, and passed it to Julie. John Henry looked over at the man and said conversationally, "I'll bet you've settled in one of those old pueblos on the cliff face. Something you have to repel into and back down out of. And come to think of it, probably got a hooch down there in the tulles somewhere close to the water. An' maybe a bolt-hole someplace else?" He paused. "You plannin' to stay up here? For the winter, I mean?"

The man smiled, but kept his peace. Clay pressed on: "I'm sure that you are prepared to hole up and tough it through, but grub this time of year is a little hard to come by, isn't it?"

The man still smiled, although it wasn't much of a smile, John Henry noted. More like a crinkle around the eyes. "Mr. Clay, it takes all the tricks in the world to make it here on the mountain, and I got tricks you never even thought of." Clay considered that but said nothing. The man continued, "This girl with the mouth. What's she to you?"

Clay looked away from the gun muzzle and into the strange gray eyes. "Her daddy is Dub Stensvahl. He's the one got himself shot. He owes me money he borrowed from me a couple of years ago. Her momma asked me to find her."

"You are not having relations? Nothin' like that?"

Clay smiled his own small smile and tugged at his mustache. "No, nothin' like that. I promised that I'd try to get her out of this country before the weather got truly bad, that's all."

"You think she's a virgin?"

"Well... since she told me that she's in the family way, she probably isn't."

"So that *was* her daddy got shot? He make it?"

"Don't know. He was alive when I left Silver." Then, "You said you saw the shooting? I mean, how he got shot?"

"Well...I didn't actually see it. I heard it all, though. From the sound of the shootin' he must have charged down the trail cuttin' loose at those guys, and like I said, they returned fire."

"They have automatic weapons?"

"Well, at least one did. Then they run for it when the trail crew came up."

That's a little different than Dub's story. Who do I believe? "Julie, where were you when this happened?" No answer. "Julie?"

"Daddy ran me off... told me to hide out... He'd come back for me."

"Did you know he was shot?"

"All I know is, after I heard the shooting I heard the trail crew yell; when I climbed back over the ridge it looked like they were already carrying him off. Then I heard the helicopter come in."

"And you decided to stay here."

"Where the hell was I gonna go? I had enough food for a while." Long pause. "Was I gonna run back to mommy and tell her I just saw daddy gunned down and, by the way, I'm preggers? Like I was thinking real clear!" Pause. "I needed some time to think."

Alan Ladd regarded the girl. "She wouldn't be too bad if she didn't have that lordamighty awful mouth on her." He cleared his throat. "So you really don't have a horse in this race?"

"Other than the thirty-five hundred her old man owes me."

Several minutes passed. Clay added wood to the fire, sat back down.

"Would you be up to a trade?" the man asked.

"Beg pardon?"

"Would you trade for her. It's plain I don't have any big money up here; what would you take in trade?"

John Henry considered. "Well sir, I don't know... I'd have to think on it a while. What have you got to offer?"

Julie perked up from her huddle in the sleeping bag. "Just what the hell are you two talking about? I'm not about to be goddam trade goods!"

"Hush up, girl. Let the man talk." She sat back, shaken. Clay continued: "Well, mister, I'm listening."

"Well, sir, I could make you a note of some kind, that would, you know, be good on the outside."

"For three thousand five hundred dollars?"

"Aw, I wouldn't think she'd be worth that much. She's not worth near that. Some cash and trade, maybe."

Julie was beside herself. "What the hell do you mean, not worth... you ugly sonuvabitch, you should be so lucky that I'd even consider being in the same room with you!" she spat at him. "You two are not going to make a deal over me."

John Henry ignored her. "Gimme a f'r instance – what do you have in mind?"

"How 'bout one of my wives? I got one that's a little younger than Missy, here, she might appeal. Just wedded her and bedded her like maybe six months ago... she don't much go for the wedded part, but she is sure happy with the bedded part. How about her and a couple hundred bucks to boot? Think she'd do?"

"Why shuck her now?"

"Aw, you know. These kids got lots of enthusiasm, but don't really know anything. A couple of my other wives none to happy about her being around. You know how it is..."

"So let me be sure I understand all this. You got a horse you need to move. You want me to buy this horse 'fore I even get to the stable – let alone have a chance look in her mouth. And how do I know that I can collect once you disappear? You go off up the mountain with the goods, I'm sittin' here with a piece of paper. Don't get me wrong, cause I know *you* would make good on it, but I don't know about your buddies."

"They would make good 'cause I'm who I am, and they are who they are. They do what I tell 'em."

"Aw, man, things change. You hide out in the Mimbres, they forget who you are, what you are... things change. I don't think so, sir."

By this juncture, Julie was practically strangling with indignation. "You fuckin' bastards have gone too far! I'm no piece of meat that you can just..." she sputtered, the words wouldn't come out.

Clay cut her off: "Julie, put a sock in it."

The man turned serious as he gestured with the Winchester, "I could just take her, you know."

"Probably you could. 'Course... that leads to all sorts of complications, doesn't it?"

"How so, sir?"

"First of all, you're not the kind that'd steal a man's rice bowl... Naw, I take you for pretty basic honest. But if you did take her, you know I'd have to come after you... so you'd have to kill me, or leave me here so's I couldn't move – be the same as killin' me. Even so, I guess she wouldn't slow you down too much, at least not at first. And she would be one more mouth to feed... up here in the dead of winter 'n' all." John Henry Clay paused with an elaborate shrug. "But you gotta do what you gotta do, I suppose."

"But I could get a start on you and be gone. You'd never set eyes on me again."

"Maybe you could," Clay said reasonably, "but then again maybe not. Agnes Two Pony will be up here tomorrow, and Eddie Sam won't be far behind. Two of the best trackers in New Mexico, maybe the world, I don't know. You and the girl will leave sign a blind man could follow, especially with her draggin' an ankle. Between the three of us we could follow you through the halls of hell." He resumed studying the fire. Julie had decided to put a sock in it.

The fire crackled and spat the resin from the pine knots. Alan Ladd pulled on his hat, shrugged into his coat, and hefted the carbine. "You're a hard man, John Henry Clay. I'd like to say I'm pleased to have made your acquaintance, but I'm not sure I am. Maybe, maybe not." Looking back at Julie, he said, "Careful with that ankle, missy," and as he slipped out into the storm, he winked at her.

Julie was wide-eyed. "Who was he? I mean, like, he stepped out of a history book somewhere."

"Unless I'm badly mistaken, he was Elder Orville Foss, of the Reformed Latter Day Congregation of the Second Coming, the gentleman my partner Eddie Sam has been chasing all over the Southwest under the enlightened guidance of the FBI."

A long silence followed, interrupted only by the fire and the occasional howl of the wind.

Finally, Julie leaned slightly toward him and said, "Mr. Clay, I have to pee."

Close Quarters

"You could'a sold me to that crazy bastard!"

"But I didn't."

"But... you were dickering with him."

"True."

"You would'a sold me? You are bigger than him. You even have a gun. You..."

"The man had a bigger gun... and he was sorta pointing it in my direction. Bigger guns usually prevail in a discussion." He rearranged her sleeping bag, draping it on the corner of a ruined wall, hopefully drying. It wasn't. "Mr. Foss just talked himself out of the deal. I figured he would when he had a chance to think about it."

He walked to the cave entry and looked out. The wind was up now, driving hard, crystalline snow on ahead of it. The overcast was beginning to break in places, but the temperature was perceptibly dropping.

"Gonna get good and cold. How's the ankle?"

"Crappy," she answered.

"Okay Julie, here is how I see things. It is already past noon, so the day is essentially lost, especially since you can't begin to walk on that thing yet. The way ankle rolls go, it might be better in an hour or two, or it might take several days. Even though this is the best shelter around, we need to get out of here. I think we can get through the night tonight if I can find enough burnable wood out there under the snow. We have to keep both of us warm and fed and it looks as though we are mostly out of food after tomorrow. Maybe we'll find help in the valley below us, but I wouldn't bet the farm on it; we need to try to get all the way out in one day's hike."

They made a supper out of odds and ends from both packs. John Henry set aside enough for breakfast then re-packed the remaining food along with the stray items she had been carrying. He knew they would have to leave anything wet behind, and that he would have to heft the major portion of the load that was to be carried out. Clay knew only too well what it was like to traverse rough terrain with even a minor injury. He'd have to carry most everything, no question about it.

Just before dark, he slipped out of the cave and down to the creek bottom. Clay selected four saplings and then cut them close to the ground using a six inch folding pruning saw, then cut them to about five and a half foot lengths and stripped them of their side branches. He carried the poles back to their shelter where he bored small holes in the butt ends, inserting in each a loop of tie-down cordage. Satisfied that they now possessed four good hiking staffs, he leaned them in a corner and regarded Julie. She was dozing in front of the fire, one arm thrust away from the sleeping bag which she had pulled loosely around her. *Innocence personified,* he thought.

"We can trim yours to fit tomorrow when you are on your feet," he announced.

She blinked. "What?"

She had taken some Tylenol earlier, he offered some again. She took them with thanks. He marked the change in her attitude; wrote it off to her injury. He inwardly feared what he knew he would have to face yet this evening.

"How's it feel now?" he asked.

"A little better, I think. Do we have any more cocoa?"

As he made her chocolate, he knew that it was time to bring up the subject he had been dreading. He couldn't put it off any longer; he steeled himself for the rebuff.

"Julie, your sleeping bag is still wet, you can't use it." He waited for the rejoinder, but she said nothing.

"We are going to have to share my bag, unless you want to rough it and take the chance of frostbite, or even freezing. It is going to be a rugged night even so, 'cause this bag is only rated to 25 degrees." She still said nothing.

"I'm sorry, but I don't know how else we can get through the night. As it is, you are going to need to put on more clothes. And we'll have to situate so one of us can reach to feed the fire."

To his utter surprise, all she said was, "Yes, sir."

He knew that while the bag was oversized to fit his 6'8" frame, it was going to be uncomfortably crowded, and the prospect of a night with little sleep didn't exactly thrill him.

He slipped into the sleeping bag first, worked his way into one side of it as far as he could. Julie would be closer to the fire, but he could reach the woodpile off to one side and, if he were careful, keep the fire fed. She got in beside him, quickly turned her back.

"Uggh. You smell," she said.

"Miss Julie, you are not exactly a bed of roses yourself."

She giggled, then said, "Good night."

A few minutes later, she said, "Were you givin' me bullshit about this Wilma what's-'er-name?"

"Rudolph. No, no bull, all true. We get back, Google her up. There is a lot more to her than what I've been able to re-member. She was really world class"

"Mr. Clay, do you think I could be good enough to be that good?"

"Julie, given another season or two, you will have Gino and Pat Summit drooling all over you."

She sighed, then he heard no more from her. It was not to be an easy night. They discovered early that in order for one to change positions, the other had to somehow accommodate. John Henry had to rise on one elbow in order to keep the fire going; it managed to burn itself down to where it was no longer heating them before he woke enough to add fuel, all of which required that Julie be disturbed also. Sometime toward morn-ing, John Henry Clay gradually awoke and became aware that he was aroused. He then discovered that Julie, in her sleep, had taken the hand he had apparently draped casually over her and used it to cup her left breast.

John Henry Clay sat up like a scalded cat. "Sweet Jesus!"

"Wha...what?" she demanded drowsily, struggling to sit up.

Clay was embarrassed to his toes. "Go back to sleep. It's nothing."

But she was waking now. "Bullshit. What's going on?"

She was sitting with some difficulty, but had come fairly wide awake at this point.

"I told you, it's nothing. Nothing at all," he said rather gruffly. "I must have been dreaming..."

She lay back down. She must have been dreaming, too, she thought. She didn't remember what about, but it seemed like it was pleasant.

Columbus NM

Hizzonor the mayor had spent the latter part of his day reaming his chief of police a new one. Actually, it was not unusual for the mayor to undertake a ream job because he found that the easiest way to deal with his ferocious temper was to turn it loose from time to time. There were two village jobs that fell within Hizzonor's hire and fire responsibilities – the first being the position of village clerk, the other being the chief. Since the beginning of his tenure as mayor, two years ago, Hizzonor had hired and fired five police chiefs, and was thinking seriously about firing this one, if only he weren't his first cousin.

He was having a beer at the San Jose that evening when his cell phone rang. It was Poochie: "You better get over here to Al's junk yard. We got two bodies. You ain't gonna like it."

"They mojados?"

"No, sir, they look like narcotraficantes. Somebody cut 'em up real bad. Stuck their peckers in their mouths."

Day 5

The Breakout

They had energy bars for breakfast. John Henry helped Julie hobble around the cave, then decided to wrap the ankle as best he could. He noted that the swelling was not too bad this morning and let her try walking with the help of the staffs he'd prepared. *Now or never*, he thought. They managed to get her shoe on, started about 8:00, later than he'd have liked. He figured they'd have another hour, maybe hour and a half of descent from the pond. It had been hard going between her sore ankle and an ice/snow encrusted trail. It took Julie a while to adjust to keeping the two staffs downhill and using them to partly support her weight. Between juggling his full pack, manipulating his own hiking sticks and helping Julie over the roughest spots, John Henry was beginning to flag. He was in the middle of steadying her as she made her way down a steep part of the creek bank when his foot slipped and he went from a half crouch down to both knees, barely arresting himself from landing flat on his face.

A raucous voice, seemingly in his right ear, screeched, "Easy there, ol' hoss. You ain't near what you once was!"

If Agnes' mystical appearance from the mists had given him a start, this nearly gave him a heart attack.

"Agnes!" was all he could gasp out.

She was leaning casually against a truck sized boulder, blanket wrapped tightly around her and blending her into the surroundings. She obviously had been gauging their progress for at least a quarter hour, never twitching a muscle.

"Girl," she said, "You don't want to work these old boys any too hard, you know. They just don't have the staying power of a young stud," and she cackled for her own benefit.

"Dammit, Agnes…"

"Girl, has this old fart been hassling you? Has he been comin' on? You tell me now and we'll go right to Sheriff Mike Noone and have the old bastard drawn if not quartered." She cackled again.

"Agnes…"

"Don't you pay him no never mind, honey," she said as she reached out to Julie and embraced her. Exasperated as he was, John Henry could only try to stifle a grin as he watched Julie smile, seemingly for the first time in two days.

Gooseberry Canyon

Once down onto the Black Run Trail, they were able to make a little better time, especially with Agnes Two Pony assisting the girl. At this lower elevation, little of the earlier precipitation had been in the form of snow. They paused after fording the Cienaga, and shared two trail bars. In response to Clay's question, Agnes said, "I waited two days for those idiots to come up here to investigate. Nobody showed. I waited for you to come back down. You didn't show. The weather turned, so I figured you had gotten yourself in trouble again, so I went to rescue you. Looks like a damn good thing I did."

Clay said nothing. Julie giggled. Agnes just looked smug.

They had just gotten past the first rockfall in Gooseberry, when Clay noticed that the two women had lagged behind. By that time he was almost to the second scramble, the easier of the two, when he missed them. When he looked back, he could see they had their heads together off a couple of hundred meters from him, but couldn't make out what they were up to. *Women!* he thought.

He decided to wait for them to make their minds up on what they were going to do before he attempted the fall. It had barely snowed along Black Run, but it was a sure thing that there had peen plenty of ice earlier in the day. The Run was bank-full, and threatening to rise still further; the three of them needed all the speed they could muster.

After a few minutes, Agnes came ambling down the canyon to him; Julie stayed where she was.

"Alright, Agnes, what is going on?"

"Just none of your damn business, Bub. Us girls got things to do. Turn around."

"What?"

"Turn around, dammit. I want to get into your pack." She started rummaging.

"I'd help if I knew what you were looking for."

"Never you mind. I'll find it."

"Agnes, damn it..."

"John Henry, cool it. You don't know anything about it, 'specially considering those 90 year old women you usually run around with!" She rummaged some more. "Ah, here we go. You gotta understand, these young things have their monthlies to deal with. She told me you'd put her tampons in here." And she walked back to Julie, whistling tunelessly.

Reserve NM Ranger Station

The meeting had ended, but the Deputy District Ranger was in an entertaining mood and he was sharing it.

"...and then he says, 'respect you in the morning? Hell, I don't respect you now!'"

He was greeted with a chorus of boos. A seasonal in the next room yelled, "The hook, the hook!" A female volunteer screwed up her face at him and said, "Boss, you ARE retiring soon aren't you?"

"Damn, you try to bring a little joy into the world, whata ya get?"

Another voice sang out: "Another day older and deeper in debt!"

"Alright you clowns, get back to work. I'll just stay unappreciated," and Frances Thomas Wilmot walked back to his office and dropped back to his desk.

Two bedraggled Indians appeared in his doorway. The larger of the two said, "Frank, we need to talk."

"Who let these two in?" Frank demanded. He was answered by silence.

"Frank," Eddie said again, "we really need to talk."

"Now what?"

They ushered themselves into the tiny office and sprawled into the two chairs in front of Wilmot's desk.

"Frank, you may recall that several days ago, you and the Feds sent us into the Blue to look for 'unusual' activity. Then you guys went off and left us to our own devices to the point where we had to hitchhike back to this dump."

"My son, ask not what your country can do for you..."

"Oh stuff it, Frank. You guys screwed us over again. We get back here to discover that the manhunt has been called off. You coulda tried to pull us out. Or something!"

"Ah, come on. You multi-skilled Native Americans live

better off the land than we poor White Eyes do in front of our TVs. Gimme a break."

Martin muttered, "I'll kill him."

Eddie sighed and said, "You want our report or not? And, why the hell did they call the whole thing off?"

"Yes. And they just called off the hunt, the warrants are still in place. Officially, no reason given. Unofficially, the girl – the one who filed the complaints – took off with her boyfriend. Seems like Elder Foss may be an asshole, but not an impregnating one."

"Shit. You wanna do the rest of this now? We got some things you might find interesting."

"Might as well, then I can actually deal with something of intrinsic value. Don't forget to do your time tickets. Then I can go back to being a poor, misunderstood public servant."

Martin said, to nobody in particular, "I *will* kill him. Slowly and with glee." The volunteer in the next room snickered audibly

Eddie spread their 1:48,000 map of the Blue on the station conference table. With a pencil, he pointed to their route in from Pueblo Park and, down Pueblo Creek and back up the West Fork. "We camped about here the first night," he said, indicating on the map. "Then we struck back over this way to about here, then kind of worked our way back to here eventually, through rain, snow, sleet and hail, I might add." He was now pointing to a spot on the wilderness boundary.

"Now, back at this place, the day before we come out, Martin was working a ridge trail that showed some tracks, when he found the body."

"Body?"

"Well, what was left of it. Lot of the bones had been dragged off, what little meat was left was mummified. We'll give you the coordinates in our report. Been there awhile. We didn't stick around too long."

"D.B. Cooper."

"What?"

"Nothing. You guys are too young. What did you do with the remains?"

"Frank," Martin might have been talking to a befuddled middle school student, "Frank, look at us. You see before you two staunch Navajo warriors, ready to deal with anything life throws at us... except dead bodies. You may recall our tribal taboo dealing with same. Don't you read Tony Hillerman, for God's sake?"

"Alright, already. Go on with your story."

"Over here, right at the wilderness edge, someone had run a bunch of cows in. We figured maybe a dozen, but could be less. Anyhow, they left those cows for a week or so to graze wilderness land, and when they moved them out they left behind a salt lick. Like they was settin' up a hunting stand. Just thought you'd want to know."

"You two are nothing but trouble. It's a wonder I have any hair left at all."

"Jus' tryin' to make a livin', Massa."

Nuevo Casas Grandes, Chih.

Several kilometers north and east of Casas Grandes, is a small, corporate owned rancho. Acting on a tip forwarded by US Customs and Border Patrol, a Mexican Army contingent of about 30 men in six camouflage vehicles descended on the rancho headquarters just before sunset. About 80 meters from the main barn, they found an open trench about five feet deep and the bodies of 32 men and women partially covered by soil in that trench. Hanging by his heels from a nearby shed, was one Carlos Bustos, late of the Mexican Customs Service. He had been emasculated, slowly eviscerated, and then hung and left to die. Several of the young troopers puked their guts up.

The Lake Road

John Henry could sense Julie's pace picking up even as his own flagged. He called a halt about a mile from the trailhead, as much to gather his own strength as to rest Julie's bad ankle. Agnes looked as though she could do a mini-marathon without batting an eye. Julie was like a horse smelling the barn, even if she was hurting.

"Agnes, how're you getting home?" he asked.

"I've got my brother-in-law's old Chevy truck. Why don't I take the girl with me? From what you say, her mom likely won't be home. I *will* take her with me." It was decided.

"Back to the Big Res? What are you going to do with her there?"

"Oh, John Henry, get with the program. My sister lives just north of Silver. We'll just stay there until momma gets back."

"She's got to get going to school again. And she will have basketball practice..."

"We'll deal with it. Give it a rest!"

They arrived at the car park just before dusk. There was one other vehicle in the lot, a muddy Hummer. Julie said, "The first thing I want to do is get a milkshake. A chocolate milkshake. Or one with Reese's Pieces in it. Yum."

"You and Agnes go on. I'm most in need of a shower; I'll grab a sandwich in Deming."

They approached Agnes' battered truck, opened the tailgate, and Clay slipped out of his backpack. Emptying its contents on the gate, he separated his gear from what was left of Julie's. He noted that all of the tampons were gone which, he was sure, accounted for some of the lightness of her mood.

"Come on, Miss Julie. We got ground to cover."

Julie turned to Agnes and nodded, then turned back to Clay. Taking his face in her hands, she went up on tip-toe and kissed him on the forehead. "John Henry," she said, "you are a cool dude."

She turned and climbed into the cab with Two Pony, and they pulled on the Lake Road, trailing a cloud of blue smoke. John Henry heaved a big sigh and thought, *Well, that wasn't much of a thank-you. Or was it? These kids today...*

He unlocked the F-150, tossed his utility belt with other some odds and ends in the passenger door, and his pack in through the third door. He did a quick walk around inspection of the truck and when he reached the rear he discovered that someone had battered the topper hatch in, leaving it hanging by one hinge. *Shit!*

It was a useless effort, since he had emptied it of anything of value. Then he thought to check the spare under the bed of the Ford. It was no longer there, its cable dangling. *Double shit!* Returning to the cab, he flipped on the lights, went back to the truck's rear and, sure enough, the tail light was not burning. This time he didn't bother with the expletive. He slipped Doc and Merle's *Deep Gap* CD into the player slumped back into the seat, and headed down 180 to home. The Deming Drive-in served him a tepid, greasy burger and the french fries were burnt. The old leg wound, which had not bothered him for several weeks, was now demanding attention again.

He tried thinking of something pleasant, like his last houseguest. He must call her, first chance he got. Maybe she was still speaking to him... Shortly after he crossed into the village of Columbus, he noted the red/blue/red/blue flashing in his rear view mirror. He pulled onto the berm, muttering. Then, for some reason, he remembered a cartoon he had seen once years ago. A man was standing with his eyes to the sky, imploring: "Why me, Lord?"

The answer came thundering down from On High: "Because you piss me off!"

He was still smiling when Chief Poochie Gutierrez shined his six-cell MagLite into the tracker's eyes and demanded his license and registration.

Day 6

April

"Frontera Tours, this is April, how may I help you?"

"April, this is John Henry. Anything going on?"

"Damn your mangy hide, J.H., where have you been? You have a bunch of calls, and some harridan with electric hair has been in here twice demanding to know where I've hidden you."

"Oh, Lord. I'm sorry, I meant to warn you about her."

"Uh huh. We have a tour wanting to go out Wednesday. They want to do the Bisbee, Tombstone bit. One overnight. I booked based on your availability. We could use a little cash flow, John Henry."

"Yeah, I should be healed by then."

"Now what have you gone and done?"

"It's a long, long story, kid. I'll take the Wednesday tour"

Refuge

The Reverend Orville Foss had spent the last three days scouting the now upscale old mining town of Hillsboro. Wanting to put distance between himself and John Henry Clay's party, in spite of the weather, he made a hurried tramp east to the Kingston Pass. Then over the divide into the silver country of the Black Range, where he hid for a day in the woods above Kingston's only bed and breakfast. Finding little to interest him in that almost ghost town, he moved on down Percha Creek to where he now lazed, carefully observing the movements of one of Hillsboro's citizens. It wasn't too much more than a ghost town. Two or three hundred people, possibly. A cluster of homes along the creek fronting the highway, and several scattered cottages and cabins out to the north and east.

She was in her late 70s, or maybe even 80s, he thought. Crisp in her movements, though, seemed completely at ease as she moved about the cabin and the rather spacious yard surrounding it. Parked in a nearby shelter was a late model SUV – Toyota, maybe – although from where he was watching he couldn't tell. Now she was hanging a meager wash on a line she had stretched from the cabin to a box elder nearby. *Nothing ventured, nothing gained*, he thought. *Here goes.*

He worked his way out to the east a bit before breaking out of the wood. Foss had already hidden his carbine and most of the goods he'd gathered from the cairn when he left the Mimbres, and figured with his wet, tattered clothing he looked as much like a trail bum as he was going to.

He stood in the clear about 75 meters from the woman, looking around in a puzzled fashion. She had noticed him, but went on with hanging the wash. Still looking slightly bewildered, he took notice of her, hesitated for a long moment, then started very hesitantly toward her.

"Ma'am?"

She looked up with interest. He kept it rolling.

"Ma'am? I'm Jay Foster; I just come down off the Divide Trail. Is this Kingston?"

"Hello there. You're in Hillsboro – Kingston is off east a bit. I'm sorry, I missed your name..."

"Yes ma'am. I'm Jay Foster. I'm a trail hiker. It's nasty up there now and I thought I'd try it down where it is a little warmer."

"Well, Mr. Foster, welcome to Hillsboro. I'm Alice Conroy. Could I interest you in a hot chocolate? Or maybe something stronger?"

"Oh, yes ma'am, cocoa would really hit the spot now. Thank you."

They certainly hit it off, the two of them; he, the youngish world traveler and she, the older, wiser mother/hostess. Foss was pleased almost beyond words as he played it low key and feigned a fatigue that he really didn't feel. After an hour of casual conversation he felt it was time for the test.

"Alice, would it be too much to ask if I could use the phone for a bit. I need to check in with my brother in Tucson. I'd be happy to pay."

"Now, Jay, don't you worry about it. The phone is right over there. Please..."

He dialed the number, carefully screening her from seeing the area code. The line rang several times before a machine answered. He left instructions for "Bruce" to call him back at Alice's number.

"Ma'am, I just don't know when he'll get the message and call back. I've imposed on your kind hospitality long enough; I need to find a place to stay tonight." He put on his best lost soul look.

"Don't you go worrying about that. We'll figure something out. Meanwhile, what would you like to have for supper?"

Orville had loaded up on the meatloaf. If this woman were 30 years younger... They talked for a bit about his "life on the trail" and about his plans for the future. By 7:30, "they" had figured out that he would unroll his sleeping bag in the corner of her storage shed at the edge of the forest, and at least spend the night waiting for his call. He had no more than returned to the cabin from that task when the phone rang. Alice answered, then handed it to him.

"Hello? Bruce?"

"Yeah. We private?"

"As can be, brother. It is real good to hear the sound of your voice. How's Ma?"

On the other end of the connection, Charlie Tree snickered. "Orville, you are somethin' else. Little Mama just misses the hell out of you. She was a-wonderin' yesterday when she'd be able to lay somethin' on you."

"Well, thank you Bruce, I'm sorry to hear Ma's not feeling up to snuff, but I guess it's to be expected. I was hoping that you might see your way clear to come over to Hillsboro, New Mexico and give me a lift home. I believe I have done run out of weather."

Charlie hesitated. "Orville, does that mean you really want to be picked up? Kin you talk plain at all? You know they called off the manhunt? They's still a couple law hanging around from time to time, but…"

"No, Bruce, I can't, and no I didn't know, but it don't change things. You know what we worked out before I left, just let that be your guide."

Alice Conroy had busied herself cleaning up from their meal, but the Reverend Foss sensed that she was tuned in tightly to the conversation.

"OK, Orville, gimme what you can."

"Un-huh. Bruce, right now I'm the guest of a special woman. Her name is Alice Conroy and she lives here in Hillsboro. Anyhow, I need to find another place to bunk until you can pick me up. When do you expect that might be?"

Alice signaled for his attention. He said, "Just hang on a minute. Miz Conroy wants to talk to me."

Alice said, "Jay, if it suits you, you can leave your bedroll right where it is until Bruce can get here. The weather is still mild down here, and I need some help around the place anyway. You wouldn't mind, would you?"

"Miz Conroy, that's might generous of you, but..."

"But nothing. You will do it until he gets here. I can't pay you much, but I can feed you good. It is settled."

He murmured thanks and returned to the telephone. "Bruce, Miz Conroy wants me to stay on here to help her out. How soon do you expect to get back from Ma's?"

"Orville, you sly dog. I don't know how you do it. She sounds kinda old for you, though. OK, so what can me 'n the boys do?"

"I'm glad you asked. I think they just sit tight until we get Ma's situation straightened out. I've got a little money and Miz Conroy's going to feed me, so I'll be alright for a bit. I'll check with you in a couple of days, see how things are goin'". And he hung up.

Alice looked concerned. "I go back to New York in, let's see, it'll be nine days, so I certainly hope you can make connections before that."

"Oh, yes ma'am, it won't be that long, I'm sure." ...*And before I leave you can damn sure bet that I will have figured a way to get back in here and spend a nice, quiet winter,* he thought.

Day 9

Confrontation

She showered first and had partially dressed again. John Henry was allowing the steam to soak into his sore muscles, singing *A Man of Constant Sorrow* through the spray. *It sounds better in here,* he thought, *but I don't think I'll ever get quite right.* She moved over to his desk to where she could see in the bureau mirror as she tucked her shirt tail into her jeans. There were a half dozen books ranging from McCullough's *Truman* to a Copper Canyon guide by someone she'd never heard of. Then she saw the letter and could not help reading it:

Kuberski, Share and Lucas
Attorneys at Law
San Francisco, Seattle, Fairbanks

Dear John Henry,

You never fail to surprise me. The three Priority Mail packages arrived here on the 10th together with your letter of instruction. You will note from the enclosed invoices that Prosser & Company ran the requested assay and sale of the materials. Their representative, Mr. A.J. Lowry, remarked on the unusually rich ore, close to placer quality. They would be pleased to continue to receive further materials. An accounting of the proceeds, including all fees including our own is herewith enclosed.

The remainder is accounted for as follows:
Net proceeds (all fees and expenses deducted)-
$12,841.64

Distribution:

>   Check #6452 enclosed,
>   John Henry Clay payee (Loan Repay) $3,500.00
>
>   Check #6453 enclosed,
>   John Henry Clay payee (Services Fee) $1,000.00
>
>
>   Check# 6454 deposited,
>   John Henry Clay & Julie Stensvahl payees
$8,341.64

We opened a joint savings account at Wells, Fargo
(passbook enclosed); please note that the signature
cards must be filled out and signed by both you
and Ms. Stensvahl and returned to the bank in the
envelope provided.

John Henry, it has been my pleasure to serve you and
hope to be able to do so in the future. Actually, I
would delight in springing you to dinner should you
find yourself passing our way. By the way, I always
regretted what we did with Don Nelson's pants. I
felt just a little guilty that we locked him out in
the hall that way. Well, maybe not _that_ guilty. Fond
memories, I think.

Deepest regards,

Woody

Elwood Franklin

   She reread it, putting it together in her head. She studied it a third time, her irritation growing.

"John Henry Clay, I believe you are a lying, scheming son of a bitch!"

"What?"

"I said, 'you are a despicable lying bastard.' You thought you were pulling a fast one, didn't you?" she demanded.

"What?" He stepped out of the shower and started drying his hair.

"You went up to the Mimbres to mine gold. You are mining a wilderness, for Christ's sake! A wilderness I am sworn to protect."

"What?"

"I read the letter from your lawyer. It's right there out in the open on your desk. You are just a cheap thief!"

"Wanda, Wanda... don't get your undies in a bunch. Look at the date on his letter. I've still got the envelope here somewhere, take a look at the postmark."

"What are you talking about?"

"Dammit, Wanda, check the dates. I had to have mailed those parcels just before I hiked into the Mimbres... the day after you were here for dinner. Remember?"

She made him check off the pertinent dates on the calendar before she could calm down. He explained where the ore samples had come from – Dub's backpack at the hospital – and how he had mailed them off from the Silver City Post Office before dropping in on her at the ranger station. Mollified, if not totally convinced she asked, "Then didn't they come from the Mimbres anyhow? If they were in his pack, and he had just been carried out of the Mimbres, it's still Mimbres gold."

"Maybe. We can't know that for sure. He will deny it, anyhow, so..." and he let it slide.

"Okay, Mr. Clay. I'll take you at your word. I'll tell you the truth, though, I don't like any of this. When I look for answers, all I get are questions. There are too many loose ends. The gold. If it didn't come from the Wilderness... And why was he shot? Who shot him. And why did he take his daughter up there in the first place? And now <u>this</u>!"

"Yeah. I wish I could help. I don't have a clue as to some of the 'whys'. I think maybe Dub getting shot was an accidental encounter, for whatever reason, I don't know. Though, 'who' shot him I might could answer... have you checked any of the guys who had wood gathering permits about then? And what was your last question?"

"Why did he take Julie with him?"

"How about this for a wild assed guess... maybe he was originally going to share his gold strike knowledge with her – assuming that was where it was coming from – but got so paranoid that he couldn't bring himself to do it. The account of the shooting that Orville Foss gave us would support that slightly, that Dub was losing it, I mean. Julie's description of their last day there didn't make it sound like he was necessarily dealing from a full deck."

He finished toweling off and reached for his tee-shirt. "A better question is, where did his gun get to? Nobody's come up with it yet, so maybe there wasn't one. I couldn't find any of Orville's tracks that could tie in, and there weren't any others, so, unless one of your volunteers picked it up on the QT..." He let the question hang there.

While she had calmed considerably, Clay could still sense the fire. *Don't know I'd like to be around this woman when she is really upset.*

Her frustration suddenly spilled: "Oh, John Henry, just...just...oh... FUCK YOU!"

"Wanda, darlin', you do have some wonderful ideas."

Years of acquired basketball reflex paid off suddenly. He was able to duck almost clear when she winged a book at him.

End Part I

Part 2

Columbus NM

Colonel Andrew Bailey founded Columbus in the late 1890s on the line just opposite the Mexican village of Palomas, and about 75 miles west of the bustling cities of El Paso, Texas and Juarez, Chihuahua. In 1903 he caused the collection of shacks that for the most part comprised the "town" to be moved three miles to the north on the newly laid tracks of the El Paso & South Western R.R. He named the town Columbus after the US Post Office refused his original request for the name 'Columbia.'

Originally established by a subsidiary of Phelps Dodge mining interests, by 1916 the EP&SW RR was running several trains a day through Columbus. The line transported the output of Bisbee Arizona's Queen Mine as well as a fair number of passengers traveling between El Paso and Douglas and various points between. Columbus found itself at the center of that trade with things looking rosy for the future.

At 4,000 feet above mean sea level, the Chihuahuan high desert had for centuries been a crossroads of Native American traffic, most recently by the Apache and Comanche. A mining boom in the Tres Hermanas a couple of miles to the west and in the Floridas, some dozen miles to the north just before the turn of the century, coupled with the expansion of the cattle industry created an importance in the area which has not been seen since. At one time, the miners camped on the northeastern slopes of the Tres Hermanas amounted to twice the population of the entire village below it.

The town's importance as a stop on the EP&SW increased over time so that by 1916 the population was about 1,300 souls. In addition to the post office, the village boasted churches and schools, a telephone exchange, a newspaper (sometimes two), several merchants, a couple of hotels, and the headquarters of the gigantic Palomas Land and Cattle Company – at one time the largest such in North America. The Army had installed a camp just south of the R.R. depot that was home to the 13th Cavalry, assigned to patrol the border. Lt. John Lucas described the town as "a cluster of adobe houses, a hotel, a few stores and streets knee deep in sand combined with the cactus, mesquite and rattlesnakes..."

Then along came Francisco "Pancho" Villa. With the Mexican revolution sputtering and his "army" greatly diminished, Villa nursed several grudges that included President Woodrow Wilson and the three merchant Ravel Brothers who he believed had cheated him on an arms deal. (The Ravels operated, among other enterprises, a "mercantile" in downtown Columbus.) Villa, with about 500 men, attacked both the local Army camp and the village of Columbus early in the morning of March 9th, 1916. Eighteen Americans, soldiers and civilians, were killed in the action. In spite of taking an estimated 150 to 200 casualties, mostly from machine gun fire, the Villistas got away with goods from the stores and a herd of army horses. In the fight, several buildings in the center of downtown Columbus burnt out.

The resulting national uproar became the 9/11 of its day. President Wilson sent General Black Jack Pershing and his troops on a 'punitive expedition' into Mexico in pursuit of the revolutionary (or terrorist, your choice). Headquartered in Columbus, the army was aided in this endeavor by such modern marvels as airplanes (represented by the army's first and only aero squadron), motor cars, four-wheel drive trucks, and Lt. George Patton, who was Pershing's aide. While this effort came to be an excellent proving ground and preparation for our entry into World War I, the eleven-month long Punitive Expedition pretty much came back empty handed.

Villa, who had been wounded, holed up in caves in Chihuahua with the help of locals for most of the time the army was searching for him. The raid did, however, almost kill Columbus. There was a burst of prosperity that arrived with the troops, but things went downhill fast when they were withdrawn. By the time of the great depression there were only about 350 people left living in the village. Those buildings that didn't burn in The Raid were torn down brick by brick and board by board and taken someplace else to be rebuilt. Today, when Columbusites think about their history (if they think about it at all) it revolves almost solely around The Raid.

In 1917 came the Great Bisbee Deportation, in which some 1200 or so striking miners there were loaded at gunpoint aboard boxcars on an EP&SW freight by Phelps-Dodge "detectives", and shipped – literally – to Columbus where the army eventually took them in. Were you to question Columbus residents today about the Deportation, all you'd get would be blank looks.

Some 1,800 souls reside in the village now, and four out of five of them are Mexican or of Mexican descent. Most are completely illiterate in English and well over half the families rank well below the poverty level. The village itself has so little tax base that 1/3 of its annual budget must come in the form of grants. There is a sordid history, if locals are to be believed, of petty graft and downright incompetence within the Village Hall. And, perhaps most sadly, the village has squandered its one chance of attracting a cash flow through exploitation of its unique history by allowing almost all the remnants of the Great Raid to disappear, as the Deportation already has. Although Columbus has a nationally designated historic district, it has been despoiled by poor remodeling and bad new building, including a "modern" post office built in its center.

By the first decade of the twenty-first century, the general area of the village of Columbus had attracted a number of Anglo retirees, most of whom discovered that living was cheap enough in the high desert that one could get along on an absolutely minimal income, and still be less than a hundred miles from big city services including a V.A. hospital. About the time of Y2K, John Henry Clay had himself discovered Columbus through the inadvertent good offices of a Navajo Indian named Eddie Sam, with whom he had worked in a Central American venture, sponsored by a certain US Government agency. Occasionally, Clay was moved to wonder at his being in New Mexico. Earlier in life he had traveled a good bit of the southwest but as a native midwesterner he had never felt moved to relocate to the desert. Yet, here he was, living in a third world village at the edge of nowhere. It was sometimes a puzzlement.

Eddie Sam had painted an enticing picture of him living the good life on the cheap and John Henry had found that it was true, mostly. Equally true was that he owed Eddie big time, and when someone had saved your life it was debt not taken lightly.

He found work as a part-time tour guide and occasionally as a tracker. He also found, as did most other citizens of the village, that they were next to – and occasionally in – a three-way border war between two rival drug cartels and the family that had controlled the local trade for as long as anyone could remember. Puerto Palomas shared the border with Columbus and served as the regional headquarters for the transit of illegal drugs, arms and immigrants flowing across the New Mexican border.

An hour to the east, Juarez was killing some five or so thousand narcotraficantes and their friends and relatives each year in a bloody narcotics war for control of the border. In Palomas, the count was comparatively smalltime and rarely reached a hundred per year, although it was very difficult to keep that count. In addition to the Sinaloa and Juarez Cartels and the extended family of Don Benito Escalara, two rival sub-gangs involved themselves in the carnage. If one added in the occasional foray by the Zetas, it was difficult at best to live in or near Palomas without being in some way touched by the ongoing bloodletting. Many Columbus residents were about to be uncomfortably involved as well.

Day 1

Spring Glory

Winter called it quits with a whimper. March winds did their usual appearance with much ado and little damage. The flanks of the Florida Mountains just north of Columbus turned a brilliant gold with the bloom of Mexican poppies, a phenomenon occurring perhaps once or twice a decade, depending on whether winter rains decided to appear. El Presidente de Mexico was threatening to move his army into Palomas to restore order – the city's police force had fled en masse into the US to seek asylum several weeks before – and worse, he was also considering sending the Federal Justice Police, the Federales, along with the army. The Federales were notorious for being hip-deep in the movement of narco-cash and arms; the agents of the US Border Patrol shuddered at the prospect of a contingent moving in just across the international line from them. On rancho land south and east of Juarez, bodies turned up, some missing heads or various limbs. In Puerto Palomas, however, things appeared to be quiet, at least for a while.

At the northeast edge of the village of Columbus, located three miles north of the convulsion taking place in Palomas, John Henry Clay had spent the morning considering the events of last November, and the eventual fallout. His friend and sometime working partner, Eddie Sam, had taken up temporary residence with him and was now putting the dishes away from a late breakfast of huevos rancheros, washed down by a large amount of coffee.

Eddie looked over at Clay and asked, "Hey, Big Guy, are you making sense of some of this crap? I get a headache whenever I try."

John Henry had been doodling on a legal pad, connecting names and places and dates. "I'm trying to do it like the guys in the detective novels. Making lists. Some of it makes sense, some of it seems like a bad crime plot... I have absolutely no idea on the 'whys' in some instances. I just know what happened."

"So, we are just a couple of guys trying to do our jobs. Where does it say we have to understand what or why. I still am trying to figure why Martin and me busted our asses up north last fall."

"You did it for the money," Clay said flatly.

"Well, there is that."

"You have any plans?"

Eddie considered as he poured them the last of the coffee. "Yes and no. I try to keep enough cash ahead so I can go walkabout for a couple of months at a time if I want to. So I'm alright there. There is a deputy job opening in Window Rock. With vet status and the amount of enforcement time I've got, I prob'ly can get on, get certified... I donno if that's what I really want to do. I'm not getting any younger – you know how that is – maybe a steady job is something I need to do. Tell the truth, though, I am kind of used to this life as a sort of nomad... it's kinda like full time RVing, I guess. Maybe it's genetic."

They sipped their coffee in silence for several minutes. John Henry said, "You need a gold strike."

"Like Dub's, you mean?"

"I was thinking more along the lines of something legal."

"There is that."

Several more minutes of silence passed. Clay seemed fascinated by the antics of a pair of jackrabbits he was watching just beyond the patio. "Dub won't talk about it. He refuses to talk to the cops, or to his ex, or even to his daughter, I guess. Did he hit a lode up there in the Mimbres? Or did those ore samples come from somewhere else? I don't know. Dub had spent a lot of time up there years ago, so it isn't like he was a tenderfoot. He knows that part of the wilderness like a book. He was a geology minor in school so it's likely he'd recognize the good stuff.

"Who fired the first shots on that trail? His daughter says he didn't, our buddy Orville says he did. And God alone knows (1) why he took Julie up there in the first place, or (2) why he disappeared for several hours each day while they were up there. We think, of course, that he was working his mine, or something like that, but we won't know for sure unless Dub talks. (3) Why, if Dub fired first on those two, or maybe three, guys, did he do it? Or, (4) if they shot at him, why? As for the 'gold strike,' what is the likelihood of stumbling onto a lode? We know that a helluva lot of mineral came out of those mountains at one time – lead-silver especially – and I suppose there is lot left, but... what're the odds?"

" 'All's well that end's well', somebody said. You got your money back. His daughter's safe, Wanda's happy, more or less. What more do you want?"

"My buddy the lawyer says I could be sued for illegal conversion of property."

"So as long as Dub's clammed up, you're safe."

Clay finished the dregs of the coffee in his cup. "I suppose so. But the questions are still hanging out there...it bothers me."

"Buddy, when you start getting a conscience, it's time for this Indian to get on the road."

Lunch

Julie had invited Clay to a practice where she introduced him to her coach and to the team. At the next practice session he attended, her coach asked John Henry if he'd mind doing a little one-on-one coaching. John Henry didn't mind, and "a little" grew to be "a lot", with Clay present at as many workouts as he could manage, given the 160 mile round trip involved.

This Saturday's session ended just before noon and Clay invited Julie to have lunch at the local drive-in. She ordered a green chili cheeseburger and fries, and he chided her, "training table food?"

She responded without batting an eye, "You bet! Coach preaches keeping up your strength, high protein, crap like that," and laughed.

"Your coach seems like a pretty savvy lady. My only experience with junior high and high school coaches has been that they were pretty jealous of their positions and resented "volunteer" help. She's not been like that." *Thank God,* he said to himself.

"I know she likes what you're doing. Technique, that kind of stuff. Myra says you've helped her foul shooting 100%."

"Those who can, do. Those who can't, teach."

"Huh?"

"Meaning, I was one of the world's worst at the foul line. Five out of ten was a good day for me."

She toyed with her fries, picking them up one at a time, dipping them in catsup carefully before conveying them to her mouth. "John Henry, what's it like to get old?"

"Ah." *What's it like to get old? Wow – I've never thought of myself as "old"… until just now.* The easy answer would be to blow the question off with something like, *I don't know, I'm not there yet,* but he felt to do so would bring an end to the closeness they seemed to have achieved over the meal.

"Girl, that's a tough one. You don't know that you've gotten there until you've passed the station." He thought for a minute more. "It's kind of like realizing that you have sort of traded being young for the understanding – call it knowledge – of what being young was all about."

"Uh huh. No, I mean like how is it physically. Like, how much do things change?"

"Some things, a lot. I can't get up on a jump shot any more, and I have eaten my step-back more than once, but that little curl/hook is smoother than ever. I can't begin to run full court for very long, but I play a decent half-court game yet. My knees are about worn out, and my feet don't move like they used to; on the other hand, I can play a lot smarter defense than I used to 'cause I have better anticipation. Does that get anywhere closer to it?"

Julie thought for a moment. "How 'bout sex? Does it change? You know, I can't picture old people having sex – no offense intended – but even my mom – yuchhh."

He thought about it. Surprisingly, her question didn't bother him, as discussion of intimate things often did. His was not a liberated home life, he knew. "Well, the 'newness' of it wears off, some of the initial excitement." He paused again. "You get better at choosing partners, and at the give and take. You get more at ease with yourself, especially when you don't have to concern yourself so much with 'The Chase.' And, he thought, *you think it's good now, wait 'til you get a chance to practice a little...*

Then, as though it had just occurred to him, he asked, "Your mom put you on the pill, did she?"

She nodded in the affirmative, and said, "Yeah, and we had the STD talk, too. I can take care of myself, John Henry."

I certainly hope so. It doesn't get any easier.

"John Henry, you played pro ball after college. Which was better... college or pro?"

"Umm. College was more exciting. Pro ball more work. Coaching means more, pays off more at college level. I like to watch the college game on TV, especially when they get into the playoffs. It's much more a team game as well as sort of a battle of wits. NBA is a lot more physical – to me that takes away from the grace of the game. Each professional team is built around a star or two and, of course, the whole idea is to make money for the franchise." He considered, "Not that NCAA ball isn't meant to make bucks for the colleges..."

"You have a favorite coach? College, I mean."

"You don't make it easy, do you. What are the criteria? And women's or men's?"

She wrinkled he nose at him. "You know, like, who do you like best... you know – the good coaches. Male or female."

"What makes a coach good? Well, of course, there's winning. Alright. Coach K is absolutely among the best, and lessee... Roy Williams. John Wooden, hands down, all time greatest, maybe... Gino; Pat Summitt, and Lute... Dr. Tom Davis, a real student of the game, his son's coaching somewhere now. Almost forgot, Bob Knight, certainly one of the all-time great teachers. Who else... can't forget Billy Nightengale, or, how about Vivian Stringer at Rutgers? That enough?"

"How about Tom Izzo? Bo Ryan?"

"Oh, he's good, time will tell just how good. Is this an all Big Ten lineup?"

"Or Rick Pitino?"

"Stop it! You're killing me. Hell, you may be one of those names someday."

She looked him steadily, "I think I'd like to be that good... there is so much to learn..."

"About everything," he mused.

"Do you actually know any of those guys?"

"Met Coach Knight on a fishing trip just before he got crossways at Indiana. Good man, sticks by his friends. Tom Davis a couple of times when he was at Iowa. I know Pat Summitt well enough to say hello, met Stringer when she was at Iowa, too. Billy Nightengale was sort of a godfather to me, helped me over some rough times – helluva guy." He thought a bit, then: "I've met some others too. Played a little city league with Denny Aye; he's out on the coast now. Oh, yeah – Kay McClain...met her through Billy."

As he was dropping her off at her home, he asked, "Heard anything from Dub? Like what he's doing now, where he's living?"

"Mom got a call from him last week. Says he is in Scottsdale, working for a mortgage broker. She said it was about time he put his education to work. Like, he was a finance major, I guess."

Finance major, geology minor…I wonder what he's up to now…

The 80 mile run back through Deming to Columbus was something he thought he could do in his sleep by now. Maybe he should move to Silver during the basketball season and be done with it. The miles were starting to wear on him. There was never a thought that he would give up his volunteer coaching, but he was beginning to wonder about his motives in helping this adolescent find herself. *I am getting old*, he thought.

What am I doing here on the edge of civilization? I could probably make more in a hundred other places. Hell, I could make twice what I bring home here. He knew, though, that he no longer thought of himself as a midwesterner; although he wasn't to the point he could call himself a New Mexican, either. *Well, I'm out here in this God-forsaken third world desert because Eddie asked me to… well, not exactly asked, but strongly invited. And I owe Eddie. A guy pulls your shot-up ass out of a firefight, you owe him something.*

What does Eddie get out of it? A good working partner…Okay, we work together three or four times a year. How about companionship? He spends more time at my place than he does at the Big Res where he has a home and million relatives. We went through so damn much together when we worked for The Company, we understand each other.

Why don't I just move down into Mexico? It'd be even cheaper. And really no different from here, much. Spanish is the language of Columbus. The only English speakers are a couple hundred Anglo retirees. The school kids don't even hear English in the classroom 'til after third grade. So the money is dollars, but that's about the only difference. And the way they do business down here on the Frontera all the money – at least most of it – goes down into Old Mexico anyhow. Damn little gets paid in taxes…

Why did I leave The Company, anyhow. Pay and bennies weren't bad. OK, I got shot up a couple of times. Ya wanna live forever? Did I quit because I couldn't keep believing in what we were doing?

A Late Call

As John Henry Clay well knew, the phone ringing after ten o'clock at night rarely bore good tidings. He had been dozing in front of Larry King when the ring tone sounded. The clock read 10:18. John Henry said, "Shit!" and, not without hesitation, he picked up the little monster.

"Hello."

"Ah, Mr. Clay himself."

"Who is this, please?"

"Mr. Clay, this is a voice from your deep, dark, devious past. You do not recognize my voice?"

"Mikos!"

"Indeed. How are you my friend?"

"Don't 'my friend' me, Mikos. Any time I have had anything to do with you it has nearly cost me my money, my freedom, or my life. Come to think of it, nearly all three the last time."

"Ah, but the adventure, Mr. Clay! Can you think of anything in your life that has brought you more adventure?"

"In a word, Mikos, bullshit. What do you want?"

"Oh, come, now. I have some things that may benefit the two of us. Be polite, pretend you like me. You can't tell me you don't miss those, ah, covert days at least a little bit."

"I'll tell you what I don't miss. I don't miss the goddamn jungle. I don't miss being shot at. I don't miss even less being shot at and hit. I like waking up in my bed each morning not missing body parts. I don't miss watching my back all the time, or..."

"Come, come, John Henry. You can't tell me that you didn't enjoy tilting windmills, fighting the good fight for good and/or evil."

"What do you want, Mikos?"

"Just a few moments of your time, my friend."

"I'm listening."

"John Henry, this involves some people in which you have an interest." The disembodied voice was unaccented but a little too precise. Talking to Mikos Constanaedes always gave him an uncomfortable feeling in the pit of his stomach. He remembered the feeling well, it was there again.

"I'm still listening."

"You are acquainted with a man called Max Cathcart?"

"The Happy Scot. The World's Most Inept Drug Dealer, Yes, I know him."

"Also, you have had dealings with a man with a Nordic name – Evenruud, Stensruud..."

"Stensvahl. What's going on, Mikos?"

"I know only that it might be to your mutual benefit to talk to a friend of mine."

"Mikos, that is simply not good enough. I am retired from all that crap. I'm out of it. I want to be left alone."

"'I vant to be alone!'" the caller mimicked the famous Greta Garbo line.

"I mean it, Mikos. I am about to hang up this phone if you can't be any more damn specific."

"John Henry Clay, your Scandinavian friend is up to his ass in something he is ill-equipped to handle. People are about to descend on him like locusts. My friend would like to talk to him, but doesn't want to go in without being thoroughly prepared. You can understand this?"

"How do I know I am not setting Stensvahl up for something?"

"Ah, an excellent precaution, as in the days of yore."

"Mikos, cut to the chase."

"Alright, my friend, I would have him contact you. His name is Tomas; he will tell you he is a contractor for J. Cairo & Sons. You should be concerned that the impact on your friends could be most unpleasant. I will tell you what... think about it for 24 hours, then call me." He dictated a number, then hung up.

Day 2

Orville

Eddie Sam sautéed the mushrooms over low heat, added the coarsely chopped scallions and finished breaking up the Double Gloucester cheese for the omelet. Clay sipped his coffee and touched the end of his cowboy mustache. "What do you hear about our old buddy, the preacher?" *Alan Ladd,* the thought came unbidden.

"Orville? I talked to Roger Jeffers the other day as a matter of fact. Asked him the same thing. He said the warrants are still in place, but since it looked like there was going to be a public relations nightmare over the girl being pregnant by her boyfriend, they called off the search for ol' Orville. They still like him for the other charges, but apparently can't justify a full blown manhunt. Or, at least the publicity around it; so says Deputy Roger."

"So he's still up in the Wilderness. Assuming he got through a bitch of a winter alive, that is."

"Oh, he's still kicking around. They apparently have enough evidence to make them think he wintered in one of those summer cabins below the lake, or maybe someplace over to the Kingston area. Makes me wonder why they didn't bother to run a check on them some time in February, but what do I know?"

"Strange guy."

"Well, yeah. Should that observation be something new?" He turned the omelet.

"No, not really. I was just thinking about him. He was for all the world the absolute Old West Gentleman when we were with him up there. Yet, he must be one of civilization's great con artists to keep those folks still believing in him."

Sam placed the egg dish on the table and said, "Dig in. Not to mention those little old blue-haired ladies who keep pitching money at him. So, waddaya think? Is he still up there? Will he try to stay this winter? Where's the Tabasco?"

"Eddie, I heard a third-stool rumor the other day that he was headed back to the Sierra Madre. I don't know. ...And the Tabasco is right behind you on the cupboard."

"So, how are you and Ranger Wanda doing?"

"Okay, guess. We see each other about once a week when she's not in Santa Fe or some other God-forsaken place. Nice lady."

Eddie tore a hot flour tortilla in half, rolled it to use as a pusher on his omelet. "You makin' any plans?"

"Not so's you'd notice. What do you hear from Martin?"

If Sam had noticed anything, including the change of conversational direction, he gave no indication. "I called him yesterday. He's alright. Went back to work at the casino last month."

"Still on security duty?"

"Naw... they are actually going to make a dealer out of him, he says. I think the boy is on to something, he'll clean up in tips."

They finished the meal in silence, until Eddie loosed an enormous belch. "Oh, yeah!" he said.

"Sweet Jesus! Don't you redskins have any manners?'

"Aw, come on. There's a lot of places where that is a high compliment to the chef."

"But you are the damn chef."

"My point exactly."

The Reverend Orville Foss was mad. Not just upset, or pissed, or even angry. He was steaming and he trying hard not let it show. "So that's the way the land lays, is it? The whole bunch of you would leave me high and dry?"

Charlie had been the messenger, much against his better judgment. "That's it, Orville. They say it's pretty simple

– either you quit runnin' and turn yourself in or we all pack up and go back to the Sierra Madre. They say they are tired a havin' the damn feds and half a dozen sheriffs sniffin' down their necks. And the do-gooders, and the child welfare bunch, and the news people..."

"You keep sayin' 'they.' What does that mean? What does Big Mama have to say in all this?"

There was a pause on the line while Charlie considered how he should answer. "She said that I could tell you that all your wives love you and will wait for you. But they are waitin' for you now and..."

"And Little Mama?"

"Well... honest to God, Orville, I know she misses you, but she misses play-time, too. You mess around out there in the wild too gosh-awful long..."

"Okay Charlie, I get the point. Where do you stand on this?"

"Now, Orville, you know that I stand right with you, whatever you want to do... ah... but I got the women to think of and they ain't givin' me no peace over all this. You got to see everybody's troubles. You just spent the winter layin' up in some widow-woman's cushy digs while we been scratchin' between food stamps and the Feds."

"Charlie, these are no cushy digs, I can tell you that. The old lady comes back from Cabo, or wherever, she's gonna know right away I stayed here – she know every dot and tiddle in that place – and sure as little green apples she's gonna run for the law. I gotta get back up to the Mimbres. I sure as the devil ain't gonna let 'em lock me up. If you all are going to run like rats, there isn't anything I can do about it. Maybe I can jack up that shyster lawyer to get the charges dropped now that they called off the hunt. One thing for sure – you all head for Sonora the Mexicans ain't gonna like you any better now than they did before."

Charlie considered. "That might be true, 'cept now they got a drug war to worry about... We're no great shakes next to that." He stopped, and when Foss had nothing to add, he said "Trouble is, you like playin' Injun up there in those mountains, as long as we can keep droppin' supplies to you now and again. And we can bring you up a little pussy in the bargain. It just don't wash no more, Orville."

"Charlie, you tell them that just like the Lord Jesus himself, I'm going to the mountain. And like Moses, I expect them by God to be there when I get back!" And he hung up the phone.

The Game

The game was at Archie Miles' place. Archie was a retired stockbroker who lived alone in a mission style
adobe at the foot of the Tres Hermanas, overlooking the village of Columbus. They met once a month, six mostly regulars,
Eddie Sam who played when he was in town, and two or three
others who played once in a while. Nobody knew how long
the poker game has been going on; there were dropouts from
time to time, and new players were admitted. Nothing formal,
nothing with any ceremony. It was nickel-dime, table stakes,
have a few beers, leave when you feel like it. If anyone thought
about it at all, he would have remarked on how much they had
in common: all the regulars were single; all either retired or
getting close; and most of them, with the possible exception of
"Cap'n Eddie," were outdoor enthusiasts. Oh, yes, and they all
had New Mexico permits to carry concealed weapons.

"The really nice thing about living in a small town like
Columbus is that when you don't know what you are doing,
somebody else always does." Cap'n Eddie was generally thought
of as the reigning wit of The South Luna County Monthly Irregular Floating Poker Club, if not its sage. Cap'n Eddie's real
name was Terrence Riordan, however that the nickname had
been acquired in honor (?) of Cap'n Eddie Ricketyback, the
owner and sole pilot of Dogpatch Airlines of Al Capp's *Li'l Ab-
ner* comic strip fame. At present, Cap'n Eddie was living in a
school bus located at the edge of an airpark just north of the
village limits. While one could describe his present situation
as primitive at best, it would do until he found an accommo-
dating female in the vicinity.

With the exception of Eddie Sam, Mamma Riordan's
only son Terrence was the youngest of them, a medium sized
man in his early fifties with flashing Irish eyes and boyish good
looks. Perhaps his only drawback was the method by which
he chose to make his living. For Terrence was a journeyman

pilot, a boomer, a Gypsy, to whom any job lasting more than a few months was as restricting as a straightjacket. Mr. Riordan had worked variously for two or three regional air carriers, on seven movie sets including *Flyboys* and *The Aviator*, for a couple of seasons at Old Rhinebeck, and even instructed students from time to time. He also worked a number of jobs outside of aviation, but what he liked most was ferrying planes from place to place.

Aircraft from Piper Cubs to Boeing 747s are moved around the country and around the world with great regularity. Besides the need to conform strictly to FAA rules in the US, a working ferry pilot must also have a full knowledge of local rules as well as customs throughout the world, have a quick mind, and endless patience. He (or she, although almost all ferry pilots are men) also must be able to endure horrible weather, terrible food, lousy sleeping conditions and ridiculous hours. "Cap'n Eddie" Riordan had paid his dues, as it were, working all over North America, and a good bit of Asia as well as a part of the Pacific Rim. In addition, one must be resourceful in the extreme in finding the means and methods of returning to one's home base. In pre 9/11 days, for instance, Cap'n Eddie would complete a ferry flight, then don the uniform of the feeder airline with which he was sometimes marginally affiliated and report to the airline gate of his choosing. Once there, he would make himself generally useful to the airline agents by comforting passengers, helping the infirm position their wheelchairs and the like. Come flight time, he would help some little old lady board, then stay on the aircraft and aid the flight crew, expecting and usually getting a jump seat allocated to him for the flight. He had just raised the pot of a seven card stud game and was bitching about nosey neighbors in general.

Archie Miles interrupted him. "I hear that the historical folks are fighting amongst themselves again. Rachel Saenz told me that the Hysterical Society has damned to hell the bunch that wants to save the old First Aero site."

Clay shook his head, "Just give Hizzonor something else to laugh at the Anglos for."

Bill James commented, "Everybody wants to be the big tadpole in this small pond. The Messicans are smart – they know what's good for themselves, but won't share it with the gringos, and the gringos know everything and are happy to share whether it's wanted or not. I'll see you and raise." He dropped a couple chips into the pot.

Roger Jeffers was thoughtful. "The average Mexican has been crapped on by his government, his patrón and his religion for hundreds of years. What it comes down to is all that matters is his extended family. Forget the rest."

Bill James looked around the table. "Stop and think about it. The gringos here – how many actually live in the village? 200 maybe? – are the only ones who care about how the village is run... or about the historical value of the place. The gringos think Pancho Villa was a miserable bandito, but every one of the couple thousand Messicans living here think he was a hero of the revolution. You ain't gonna change that any more than you are gonna change their attitude about how Hizzonor and the gang run this dink-water town!"

"Everybody's looking out for Number One, Anglos too."

"If that's so, how come some of these folks can live next door to a drug operation for months and never notice it," demanded Eddie Sam. "I'm in."

Jeffers said, "The defense rests."

A few of the players snorted. Joe Ramirez threw in his hand and commented, "You will all be happy to know that the Gov announced today that he's sending a bunch more National Guard down to aid us understaffed Border Patrol guys. No idea how many, or where they will house them."

Deputy Roger Jeffers added his hand to Ramirez', "They are going to open that temporary camp over by Hachita. We just got a grant to step up patrols along the Border Road, by the way. You might want to watch it; like, you know – like, cut it back to 20 over."

The pot went to Eddie Sam. He carefully pulled the chips across the table to his growing stack. To Ramirez, he said, "Heard you guys pulled two more out of the desert yesterday. Mojados or mules?"

Joe considered, "Neither, from the looks of 'em. Looked like executions again. Usually they keep all that stuff on their side, but for some reason it's been spilling over."

"Deal the cards, will ya?"

Jeffers said "Sheriff thinks somebody is sending a message. Won't be the first time."

John Henry Clay finished the shuffle, and announced: "Five stud, one-eyed jacks."

"I tell you what, boys, what somebody really needs to do is something about those damn Messican wetbacks. Used to be you could hustle them off the place and they'd leave –'Sí, Señor, sí Señor.'... now, dammit, the other day a couple of them took a shot at one of my foremen!" Bill James had pretty much turned control of the ranch over to his son a year ago, but still worked every day. "I told 'em, next time, shoot back."

"Suppose the fence gonna do any good?"

"Nah. I'm sure you heard that the governor of Chihuahua is real pissed about how those reserve Seabees screwed up, didn't you?"

Bill spoke up, "I'm surprised; those boys got everybody laughing at them. Put in a couple hundred feet of that damn fence following the old ranch fence line. Didn't use GPS, nothing. Ended up a few feet inside the State of Chihuahua. International incident."

There were scattered guffaws around the table. They had all the regulars tonight plus Eddie Sam. "Ugly damn thing," he said.

Bill James said, "That fence line was run by the Palomas Land and Cattle ten years before Christ. Nobody complained 'til now."

Joe Ramirez put in, "If they were going to build the fence the entire length of the border – and maybe add booby traps and punji sticks – it might work. You suppose those damn bureaucrats figure the wets won't find the ends of it and just walk around?"

"Everybody anted?"

In the course of the conversation, Terrence Riordan came to a realization. By no means an epiphany, it nonetheless came as a mild surprise. It startled him because he had not been aware if it in all the time he had known Eddie Sam and John Henry Clay.

Sitting in a room with these men of average size, Clay did not seem out of place. One did not notice how much taller he was than the others although even when seated he had half a head on them. On the other hand there was Eddie Sam. When Eddie entered a room one had the sense that he was filling it. Riordan was sure that if you asked a bystander who was the taller, Sam or Clay, that benighted individual would have to pause and think about it. Clay fit into his surroundings, Sam dominated them.

In a sense, Riordan postulated, they were the Odd Couple. They had known each other in some past life – Central or South America he thought, where they served (was that the right word?) together in what was probably the CIA. Clay was the more taciturn of the two, but both were ice-pick sharp. They were good friends to those close to them but Terrence decided they could be bad, bad enemies to someone if they so decided. Eddie Sam was energy in a keg-like body; John Henry Clay was strength. Interesting, he thought.

At that point, Deputy Jeffers' radio squawked. He listened intently for a brief minute, then announced, "Gotta go, gentlemen. Sounds like Hizzonor's found a body at the Village Hall."

When the game broke up a half hour later, Clay and Sam climbed into John Henry's pickup and headed for Clay's trailer, where Eddie Sam had spent his last two nights on the fold-away sofa. Neither commented on Roger's radio call.

"Hungry?" Sam inquired.

"Naw. Where'd we go, anyhow? Sidewalks rolled up a couple hours ago. Got cookies and milk at the house."

"Hey, is it true what I hear about your old buddy Dub?"

"What's that?"

"I heard that he's turned honest and working in Phoenix."

"Yeah. Actually, Scottsdale; he's working as a mortgage broker, according to his daughter."

"In Snotsdale? I thought you said he was doing something honest. Mortgages, huh."

Clay considered a moment. "It takes all kinds, buddy, it takes all kinds."

Turning off North Boundary onto Nimbus Rd., Clay slowed to accommodate the washboard gravel. "The little girl has done well, though. Her team has gotten as far as the state semi-finals. She's going to be good, assuming that her dad leaves her alone. Her momma's about half nuts after that shooting, and I guess I don't blame her; she refuses to let Dub have unsupervised visits with her." What he almost added, but didn't, was that momma had also started Julie on The Pill.

Eddie said carefully, "She gonna be alright? Seemed like a nice kid under all the anger."

Clay sighed, "I hope so... actually, I do think Julie will survive OK. She doesn't sound like a mule skinner every other word, at least most of the time. She's trying to quit biting her nails. Her grades are up, some. And, maybe most encouraging of all, she is working her buns off to learn the game... and she is seeing some payoff on the effort."

John Henry carefully hung his battered Celtics cap on the peg next to the back door and noticed that the phone message light was blinking. He hit 'playback.'

"John Henry Clay. Please call me back as soon as you receive this message. It is most important. Use the number I gave you earlier," and the caller hung up.

"Who the hell was that?"

"Do you remember Mikos? In Honduras, the first time?"

"No shit. What's going on?"

"I donno. The man scares me." He dialed the 888 number Constanaedes had left with him, and switched to speaker phone.

Three rings, then: "J. Cairo and Sons." *A real, live person!* Clay thought. He asked for Mikos and the voice responded, "Mr. Constanaedes is not available at this time. May I ask who is calling?"

"This is John Henry Clay, returning his call."

"Thank you, Mr. Clay. He asked that you wait by your phone for his callback."

After he hung up, Clay turned to his friend and said, "Something's up. Whatever it is, if Mikos is behind it, I better check my insurance policies."

"What's with the 'J. Cairo and Sons?' What kind of a front is he running now?"

"Ah...who knows. If I know him, I'd bet it's his idea of an inside joke. I was thinking about that. Mikos is a movie nut... you remember the Peter Lorre role in the *Maltese Falcon*?"

"The little fairy. Gardenias."

"That's the one. In the movie his name was Joel Cairo. It's just the kind of tongue-in-cheek thing that Mikos and who-ever he's working for now would come up with."

Eddie mused, "CIA?" He paused, "No, wait – come to think of it, wasn't he once Mossad, didn't we figure?"

After a moment, Clay said, "He was for hire. Well, hell... we all were for hire, weren't we?"

"Them was the days, buddy," replied Sam, "them was the days." There was just the faintest gleam of nostalgia in Eddie Sam's eyes.

Sam made himself an onion sandwich and opened a Diet Pepsi. John Henry had the maple cookies out and was pouring a glass of skim milk for himself when the phone rang. He picked it up and said, "Hello?" and flipped it to speaker again.

"John Henry." A statement, not a question.

"Mikos, I have Eddie Sam with me. You are on speaker, so he can hear also."

"Ah, Mr. Sam, the huge Navajo warrier. How are you, my friend.?"

"Still riding up front so far, Mikos. What's happening?"

"So as to not waste words, gentlemen, it seems that some things have gone awry."

"Mikos, what does that have to do with me? Or us?"

"You will recall me mentioning my friend Tomas to you, John Henry. He was killed tonight. Left on the doorstep of the Village of Columbus, so to speak. Actually, tortured and then left to exsanguinate in his car, to be absolutely correct about it. I am told that the torture was nasty. He would have given up any and all of his contacts. That would include you, Mr. Clay, even though he'd never talked to you."

They exchanged glances.

"Were I you, John Henry, I might at least watch my back for a while, assuming I didn't seek another climate."

"Mikos, what the hell have you done to me? And what the hell is going on? You miserable old con man, you owe me that much."

"John Henry, you know that in our business expediency rules all. I have never led you astray except out of need, and I think you must appreciate that. I could have just as easily chosen not to warn you about all of this, so understand now that what I tell you is true.

"I don't know where your Scotsman, this Max, fits into this – if he fits at all. Tomas only mentioned him in passing. However, your Viking friend seems to be a magnet for problems. He apparently was involved at one time in a money laundering scheme that has brought about his present troubles. Tomas seemed to think he could be, ah... an asset in prosecutions. I cannot tell you more than I have because I don't know any more."

"Mikos, just for the hell of it, if I asked who your employer is these days, would I get an answer?"

"Certainly. It would be one you would not care for, I am sure. As they say, '...then I'd have to kill you.' However, I shall tell you this much: I am basically self-employed again and aligned with the forces of good, for the most part. I might be able to assist in the future, or perhaps not. I can be reached at the number I gave you. If I do not choose to return your call, you will understand, I am sure."

"Just tell me this, Mikos, will Tomas have a replacement?"

"Possibly, my friend, possibly not. I must go. *Bon chance* to you both." He disconnected.

Eddie Sam and John Henry Clay looked at one another. *What now?* hung unasked between them.

Day 3

A Tracking Lesson

Martin Begay studied his sister's middle son from the corner of his eye as they sat in the shade of a juniper. The desert was beginning to heat up below them; behind them on the north faces, snow still lingered in pockets. Wayne was anxious to demonstrate his newfound tracking skills and Martin was grateful for an excuse to get out of the house, and frankly, away from the smoky confines of the casino.

They had taken a break to munch trail bars and to absorb the scenery about them. Martin had let his nephew take the lead and he was just about to suggest they do some paired tracking, with one of them following a track and the other cutting trail ahead.

The kid was a little above average in both height and intelligence, Martin thought. He'll be, what, a senior this year? If you overlook the acne, he was good looking; he certainly was interested in learning to track and had a lot of the fundamentals down pat. Wayne washed the last bite of trail bar down with a swig of water and turned to his uncle. "Martin, you and Eddie talk about situational awareness. I think I understand, but I'd like to go over it again, if you don't mind."

"Sure. You drive on Interstate 40, that's a situation you can probably clearly picture in your mind. It's different than driving the washboard to your Aunt Thelma's place. Why"

"Well... whole other rules apply. Completely different sets of exposures."

"Yeah, but the basics are the same, aren't they? You still have to control the car within, ah... its environment. And you do it without thinking about it, you are just aware of where you are and what you are doing."

Wayne nodded agreement. Martin went on, "Down there on the flats you can sort the tracks by what critter makes them just like you do up here, but you can be fairly sure that you won't find bear tracks down there, because bear don't – as a rule – don't run in the desert. So you just know what to expect in grassland and up in the pines. You've followed enough deer sign that you can pretty well figure where the doe will go, what happens when she's startled, where she'll bed down and where she will take her nap during the day. That's being aware of your quarry. I've seen trackers who followed sign for a few dozen feet, stopped and pointed off someplace else and said, 'Thar she blows' or something like that. They knew, because they understood their animal. Not much different tracking humans, either."

Wayne said, "Uh huh." There was a kind of challenge to his stuff he was beginning to find appealing.

Martin smiled, said, "OK, let's do some real tracking. How about that coyote we saw earlier over there? Let's see how far we can leap-frog him. Go ahead and find us a starter."

After several minutes, Wayne called out, "Tally ho!"

"Okay, hold your position for a bit." Martin trotted to where the youth was standing. "Tell me what the situation is."

"He's walking. The prints are about a foot or a hair more apart. I know it's a coyote because the tracks line up. And see here, he has a broken nail on the left hind foot."

"How do you know it's the left hind? And tell me, how do you know it is a he?"

"Well, it's the smaller print and on the left side. And I don't *know* he's a male, he just looked like it."

"Alright. Now, you go ahead and see if you can cut his trail, oh, say about 10 or 15 meters up the way. I'll work it from here."

"Uncle Martin, how come you guys use the word 'meters' but don't use metric for anything else?"

"Donno. Maybe it's the military beat it into us. Clicks and meters. I'll have to think about it."

Begay had almost caught up to his nephew when Wayne yelled, "Here we go. I got him."

"OK, stay with his trail, and I'll try to cut it up ahead."

"Got him. And look here, we've got company." Wayne examined the trail. "Yeah. Another coyote intersects right here. I'm betting it's a female, 'cause look how the other one jumps in behind. Goes right to a lope – see how the stride lengthens? And I know he is following her because his track is on top of hers here and here..."

"So, how old is your 'female' track?"

"Huh?"

"Get your head on down there where you can scan *across* the tracks. Then ask yourself, 'How long ago did we have a good wind? Or if there was no wind, have the tracks started to decay anyhow?'"

"Yeah... her tracks are still sharp at the edges. So recent passage... it was windy yesterday afternoon."

"Very good! That, bud, is situational awareness. Go ahead and track, Wayne. Be sure you keep the tracks between you and the sun; getting' close to time when the sun'll be too high to help us. You keep cuttin' trail and I'll mark for you." *Yessir, the kid was beginning to get it.* Martin smiled a smile of deep satisfaction to himself.

Day 4

Mad Max

Max Cathcart lived in the wrong era. He pictured himself as the last of the freebooters, a strong, silent type who swept the world before him. He knew he was handsome, had money (usually) and had the demeanor of an innocent (when he wanted to). He was almost six feet tall, with sandy hair and Paul Newman blue eyes, and a soft, slightly English accent. Lately he was not quite as careful as he once was about his appearance or his toilette, but he could still be quite presentable. It was known that he was a full-time RVer who moved about on the border every few months, as whim took him. Most recently he had arrived in Columbus driving an old road warrior, a decrepit Winnebago. That he had acquired a reputation from The Big Bend to Ft. Huachuca he felt was something to be proud of. Unfortunately, his major claim to fame was as the *World's Most Inept Drug Dealer.*

What was known about Max Cathcart was that he seemed to have a steady source of income, had worked a couple major southwestern cities as a small-time pimp, and sometimes, seemingly without effort of his own, he could create chaos in the lives of those unlucky enough to count him as a friend. He had attempted several times to break into the drug trade with notably disastrous results. As was once observed about Bill Clinton, Max, in his own small way, brought with him his own personal shit storm.

Had Max been born in the day of the British Raj, his family could simply have banished him to the sub-continent with the rest of the "Remittance Men"; and having done so, would have forgotten about him, were it not for the continued obligation of providing a stream of checks for his maintenance. Max had cheated his way through Sandhurst, lost a small fortune for his family's bank, presented his father with two babies from the wrong side of the blanket, and had been banished for his efforts to the Colonies for the rest of his father's life. In short, Max Cathcart was a sociopath, albeit he could be a likeable one at times.

While it must be said that Max Cathcart was not the brightest barb on the wire, in all fairness it must be noted that he was not without talent. After one youthful adventure, Max had been unceremoniously shipped to Gairloch on the Isle of Skye. There he was placed in the none too tender hands of one of the MacCrimmons, a master of that apparatus most resembling a stuck pig – the bagpipes. He proved to have some aptitude for the pipes, which in his family's view, was about his only redeeming quality. When the MacCrimmons returned him to the shelter of his family, with – it must be said – some rather inelegant complaints from the fathers of various lasses, it was recorded that The MacCrimmon himself shed tears. Whether from sadness or joy was not recorded.

His crowning achievement in Columbus was to turn out the entire village police force along with the volunteer fire department one brisk 3:30 AM with his somewhat alcoholic rendition of the *coel beag*. The coel beag, he tried to explain, was the lighter music of Scotland, but Poochie, in consultation with Hizzonor, light or not, impounded the offending instrument for several days.

Someone in the Poker Club once pressed Deputy Jeffers on why the Columbus area attracted so many nut cases. Roger replied, "Oh, no. You don't understand... Santa Fe is full of crazies, what we have here are *eccentrics*." He went on to explain that while we complained long and loud about the many fringe dwellers who made up the Frontera, our English cousins actually cherished their eccentrics. We simply needed to appreciate them more. He had not, at that point, met Max Cathcart.

Max had established himself in Frontera lore by his attempts to enter the drug trade. He found that while it was fairly easy to purchase the goods at a retail level, 'respectable' narcotraficantes were reluctant to sell to someone they did not know well. Unable to show a profit on such a small scale, Cathcart decided to enter the trade in a bigger way. What he decided to do was to make larger spot cash purchases in Mexico, bring the dope into the US, and then sell the drugs on credit. He had made what was for him, a major marijuana buy, then circulated the Bisbee-Douglas-Willcox area of Arizona to sell the dope. He had decided to unseat the two major dealers in the area by allowing his prospects a credit line. Unfortunately, he discovered that users do not care to pay for anything once it was used. Credit, it seemed, was not a good idea.

When that enterprise went up in smoke, so to speak, he took another try, this time with a Mexican partner who was to make the actual purchase. Max, having given his partner the money, was to meet him following the buy to make the goods transfer to Max's new SUV just outside the Sonoran border town of Naco. He began to suspect that something had gone awry when, at the appointed time, his partner did not show. Instead, several hours later, another Mexican arrived with the news that the shipment had been delayed by a breakdown, but that he would simply take Max's Suburban and make the pickup. Sorry, Max would have to wait in Naco because the villains he was dealing with did not trust Gringos. When the second Mexican had not returned by the next afternoon, Max was forced to walk back across the border and call a cab from Bisbee. The Suburban turned up in Juarez two months later.

For some reason known only to the Almighty, Cap'n Eddie had learned to tolerate Max Cathcart, and Max in turn, went out of his way to help Riordan with the necessities of life on the Frontera: Tecate, tequila, girls and the occasional joint. Perhaps it was their shared Celtic heritage. Cap'n Eddie had taken temporary employment as a lineboy at the Deming Airport, some 30 miles north of Columbus, in the hope of making a contact or two. While pumping gas and wiping jet windshields was not what he considered highest and best, he didn't mind. He knew that fortune smiled on those Irishmen who made known their availability for better things.

Two occurrences made that day memorable for Terrence

"Cap'n Eddie" Riordan. The first was innocuous enough; Riordan watched a Citation jet land on runway 28 and taxi in to the ramp where he hand-signaled the pilot into a parking slot. The airstair door opened as he chocked the nosewheel, and three men emerged. It seemed to Cap'n Eddie that he had seen one of the men before. He was in his 50's, darkly Hispanic and in a hurry. Riordan took a fuel order from the pilot and ordered up the fuel truck. He then entered the cabin of the plane with a large plastic bag to so that he could empty the ash trays and waste baskets. As he cleaned up the cabin he found a small cell phone under one of the passenger seats, picked it up and walked briskly to the FBO office, where he found two of the passengers in deep conversation with a third he hadn't seen before. Riordan decided his target was the older Hispanic, so went out to the parking lot where he found him about to board a new Chrysler.

He approached the Hispanic. *"Señor, por favor..."* and he handed him the cell phone.

The man's reaction was interesting, Riordan thought. At first his face showed disbelief, then anger, and finally a sort of relief. He thanked Cap'n Eddie profusely and tried to press a twenty dollar bill on him, which Riordan refused.

"Well, sir, you have my gratitude. If I can be of service to you ever, I am in Palomas." He extended his hand, "Benito Escalara at your service."

To which Riordan replied, *"Mucho gusto, Señor, a Sus ordenes. Terrence Riordan."*

"Mr. Riordan, your courtesy is appreciated. I hope to someday meet again." He got into the car, followed by another who had apparently been standing in the shadows. Cap'n Eddie marked the man with interest – probably Mexican, slender, medium height, and certainly to be noted, wearing a gun under his jacket available for a left hand draw.

Riordan now was able to place Sr. Escalara as the head of the local reputed drug trafficking family.

The second occurrence of note was when he and John Henry Clay were approached by Max Cathcart as they ate an early dinner in Columbus at the Tres Amigos Restaurant.

Cap'n Eddy was demolishing a plate of New Mexican enchiladas, *verde, por favor*, and Clay was working his way through the owner's famous *tomatales*. The interruption was not especially welcomed but nonetheless they invited Max to share their table, one of only five in the place.

Cathcart spent the next hour regaling the two with his most recent exploits, and they listened politely. Max then announced that he had an astounding surprise that he would be delighted to share with the others. He extended an invitation to both to accompany him to Palomas where he could share his good fortune with them. Clay, who would have ordinarily discovered an appointment in Santa Fe or some other remote location, was intrigued if only because of his earlier conversation with Mikos Constanaedes; and Cap'n Eddie agreed to go (1) because Clay was going, and (2) because you never could tell what Max would turn up, legal or otherwise.

They parked on the Av. Cinco de Mayo, about ten blocks south of the border crossing. Avoiding two Tarahumara boys begging *dulces* the trio entered a low, two story ramshackle apartment. Mounting a failing staircase reeking of mixed cooking smells and marijuana smoke, Max halted in front of a door halfway down the hall and produced a key. "I just rented the place. It's about as good as it gets here," he reported with a happy smile.

Their eyes gradually adjusted to the low light and they found themselves in a rectangular room about 12 x 16, with a few beat up chairs arranged without order against the near wall. There was a glowing lamp toward the other end of the room, positioned just short of a second doorway. Besides the chairs, a tiny wardrobe stood against the long wall next to what appeared to be a small sofa. Cathcart motioned for them to seat themselves on the chairs, and walked to the far door, knocked once and let himself in. He reemerged after a few minutes, soft music now playing behind him.

"OK, gentlemen, watch this."

The door slowly opened inward and nothing happened at first. Then an apparition in silk seemed to fill the doorway, moving and swaying in time to the music. John Henry realized he was holding his breath. Off to the side, Max switched on a handheld spot which he held on the gyrating figure, now revealed to be a slip of a girl in vaguely oriental dress. She moved sinuously to the increasing beat of the music, then began losing parts of her costume, slowly stripping to a chemise and thong. A few flourishes and these went as well. She then assumed a series of revealing poses, going slowly from one to another. She appeared to be Asian, quite young and nubile. And as nearly as Cap'n Eddie could see, with a perfect body.

John Henry, who had been standing throughout, staggered a half step back and fell onto a chair. "Sweet Jesus," he murmured.

The girl bowed, still quite nude. "You like, Joe?" she asked sweetly.

Terrence Riordan struggled for breath. "Mother of God," he said almost to himself. "Where did she come from?"

Max literally pranced to the center of the room. "Isn't she something, boys? She is Thai, and as you can see, well practiced in her trade. I bought her a few days ago in Hermosillo. Her name is Hsu."

Neither of the 'boys' had totally recovered their voices. Cap'n Eddy broke the spell, "She's Thai... and you bought her...? How in the world..." He couldn't finish.

"She had a 'manager'; I gave Hsu $10,000 to buy her contract out, then just whisked her up here. I'll make a fortune!"

Riordan: "You gave HER ten grand?"

Cathcart: "Absolutely. Isn't she just something, though?"

Riordan: "Ten grand."

Cathcart: "And worth every cent of it, I assure you"

Riordan turned to the girl, who stood beaming in the altogether, and asked her name in English. She stood taller and beamed some more. He repeated the question in Spanish and she replied this time with the Mexican equivalent of "You like, Joe?"

Clay, beginning to recover from the initial shock, sensed an impasse developing.

And then, Cap'n Eddie, with a flash of brilliance that

separates lineboys from jet pilots, launched a question in a sing-song totally unknown to Clay. The girl brightened even more, and gushed forth for several minutes, only occasionally interrupted by Cap'n Eddie. As she scampered from the room she threw Riordan a big kiss.

"Well," said Cap'n Eddie.

"What, sir, was that all about?" demanded Max.

"Max, she is Thai, but as you saw, speaks passable Mandarin. However, I should point out that there is a sort of, well, small glitch."

The Scot raised a slightly shaggy eyebrow, "And that being..."

"The ten grand? She says that was your personal gift to her in admiration of her talent, which, incidentally, she described in some detail. Interesting to say the least."

"Gift? What gift? It was her purchase price."

"Maybe you didn't explain the situation very clearly to her. At any rate, you owe an Hermosillo pimp whatever the going market is for a very accomplished Thai young lady. And, I have absolutely no idea where your ten thousand is."

As they crossed the border and pulled up to the customs-check lane, Clay turned to Riordan. "Are you thinking what I'm thinking?"

"I don't know. I kinda think that if I were Max, I'd be picking up travel brochures."

Clay's brow furrowed. "That pimp has lost all sorts of face over this. Circumstances don't matter, all he will care about is making Max pay, and not just in dollars."

The customs agent examined their passports, gave them the usual bored quiz and they were allowed to pull out to the highway. "He will kill them both, won't he?"

John Henry sighed and said, "Max is a dead man. Her pimp will probably beat the crap out of her and put her to work in a crib somewhere, if he doesn't kill her outright"

"I suppose that even a dickhead like Max doesn't deserve that."

Clay turned to Riordan and asked, "What the hell can we do? He's made his bed, let him lie in it."

"Uh-huh. It bothers me. Nobody really deserves that. Besides, who would we have to play the pipes at your funeral?"

"So?"

"So lemme think about it."

John Henry smiled his faint smile. "Well... give me a call if I can help."

As they slowed to the 35 limit for the Village of Columbus, John Henry asked, "I know I'm going to regret asking, but how in the hell did you learn to speak Mandarin?"

Practice

"Well, OK... nice shot fake. But let's look at that move, part by part." Clay was working with two of the girls at one end of the court while the rest of the team went through a half court scrimmage at the other end. He handed the ball to Luna again, "Let's do that over again, step by step."

With Maria guarding her at the foul line extended, she did a little fake to the left, stepped through to the right with a dribble, then did three more dribbles eventually turning her back to the basket, picked up the dribble, faked right then pivoted left for a little push shot. This time it was blocked.

"Luna, gimme the ball. OK. Now, Maria has several inches on you, doesn't she? That's a consideration, but if you post your guard properly it won't make too much difference. I'm going to start from the three point junction with the foul line extended like you did and move into the post, but with only two dribbles. By that time I will either be in a position to make a move or I won't. It is important that you be aware of how your guard is playing you, though."

He flipped the ball to Maria, and she tossed it back, starting the play. He made a small fake left, stepped through toward the basket, dribbled twice, then picked the dribble up with his back to Maria and the goal. As a part of the same motion he barely dipped his right shoulder as though to move to the right; instead he pushed off his right foot, rolled to the left, his right arm coming up as though for a hook shot. As Maria moved with the fake hook, he stretched out his left arm with the ball and, in rhythm, reached under her outstretched arms and finger rolled it at the basket. He didn't bother to see whether it dropped; both girls stood there agape as the ball fell thru the hoop.

It was purely a showboat move, right out of the Trotter's playbook. He didn't know why he did it, he just did it. Maria retrieved the ball, uncertain what to do next. John Henry simply said, "Now let's see you do a post-up move on Luna."

Clay drove Julie home after practice was over. She didn't say much, still in a slight glow from the locker room chatter about her mentor's big-time move to the basket.

Day 5

Don Benito

Cap'n Eddie Riordan spent a mostly sleepless night stewing about Max Cathcart and what seemed a fore-gone conclusion as to the remainder of the Scot's life. At nine o'clock, he put in a call to the Pink Store, and asked for Luis, the restaurant's Segundo. After a brief conversation he hung up, called the fixed base operation where he worked at the Deming airport and begged off sick. He bathed as best he could in a basin, shaved and put on his best slacks and short-sleeved sport shirt and polished his loafers. At noon, he left his school bus abode and drove to Columbus' Main (and only) Post Office where he picked up his mail (a bill from the Columbus Electric Co-op, a letter from an ex-wife's attorney, the monthly maga-zine from the Aircraft Owner's and Pilot's Association, a blurb from AARP, and slightly perfumed letter postmarked Hono-lulu), and cornered Rick, the Postmaster, for a brief chat. He then went to the First New Mexico Branch next to the Village Hall where he cashed a check for his last (almost) hundred.

Noting the time as 12:42:03 PM on his pilot's chronom-eter, he then drove south three miles to the border parking lot where he left his car and strolled into the Republic of Mexico. He bid the *adueno* agent a *"Buenas Tardes"* and wandered the long block down Avenue Cinco de Mayo, through the vari-ous street vendors and begging Tarahumara children. At the square containing a giant statue of Pancho Villa on a rearing stallion, he turned left, crossed the street to the Pink Store, which, indeed shimmered its brilliant namesake pastel in the midday sun. As a tiny Indian woman named Marcelena held open the door, he strode in as though he owned the place and greeted Luis.

Luis extended his hand and said, *"Como esta, amigo?"*

They shook in the Mexican style. *"Muy bien, gracias."*

Luis seated him at the side of the main dining area; the waitress approached to take his order. "Not right now, Marta, but I will have a Coke."

By 1:30 the lunch patrons, mostly Anglos he noted, were beginning to clear out and the local Mexican business-men – those who thought they could afford the menu – began to arrive. At 1:51: 36 by his chronometer, a rather short, broad, swarthy man entered the dining room, swept it quickly with his eyes, and nodded to Luis. He, in turn, stepped into the waiting area and returned with Don Benito Escalara in tow. Luis seated them across the room from Riordan. Terrence noted that both sat facing the entry.

Shortly thereafter, Luis stepped up to their table again, and whispered to Don Benito. He nodded, then whispered back. Luis nodded gravely, walked directly to Riordan's table. "Don Benito says to tell you that he must refuse your kind offer; instead he asks that you join him."

"Mr. Terrence Riordan, we meet again. Please, if you have not eaten, join my comrade and me, will you not?"

"You are most kind, Sr. Escalara."

"Please, no formalities. Are you more comfortable if we speak English?"

Cap'n Eddie had learned long ago to stay with his native language whenever he could, even though he had a working grasp Spanish. "Thank you, Don Benito."

"Terrence Riordan, please to meet my associate, Emilio."

"Mucho gusto," they shook hands across the table. Emilio's eyes met his only briefly, then resumed sweeping the room.

"Emilio, Mr. Riordan is the man at the airport I told you about. Forgive an old man's curiosity, Terrence, but I believe I heard the mention of a sobriquet – was it 'Captain Eddie'?" He ordered drinks for the three of them.

Terrence had the grace to look almost as though he would blush. "My friends, Don Benito, have decided that I bear some resemblance to a comic strip character of that name." *He's checked me out, and this is his way of letting me know.*

Emilio Treviso seemed almost disinterested in the newcomer at his table, but the fact was, as Riordan was aware, that he was examining his every move. Don Benito raised his glass in toast to the two others, "To new friends and old."

Escalara said, "Your name would make me think you are of Celtic origins, perhaps?" He pronounced it KEL-tic.

Riordan smiled broadly, and in his best County Limerick brogue, said "Even so, your honor, as ever was!"

This time even Treviso risked a small smile.

During the meal, they talked of business conditions in Columbus and in Palomas. They chatted about flying and the business of non-airline commercial aviation. They even, to their mutual surprise, discovered an affection for the old John Wayne movies. When the table was cleared, Don Benito offered cigars around. They lit up, Don Benito saying, "I have this feeling, Terrence, that this meeting may not be as serendipitous as it first might seem."

You bet it isn't, you old fox. "I am an open book to you, sir. I actually hoped to seek your counsel on a matter that affects some people I know."

Escalara nodded wisely.

"A man who would be my friend has, to put it in the vernacular, caught his tit in a wringer. You probably are aware of Max Cathcart."

Escalara and Treviso exchanged glances. "Mr. Cathcart and I have met. He has an unfortunate reputation." He paused, then, "You and the tracker, Clay, met with him yesterday, I believe."

He's already a mile ahead of me. "Yes sir. Well, to try to shorten a long story, I have heard that you have been known to take an interest in, ah, certain young people who, ah, show promise. With this in mind, there is a young lady, a most attractive – and talented – young lady who has been brought to Palomas by Mr. Cathcart. I might add, sir, that I consider her breathtakingly attractive."

Escalara looked at Emilio, who nodded strongly in the affirmative. "Go on," he said.

"There has been the kind of mix-up that I used to think happened only in cheap comedies," and he went on to explain the situation to Don Benito.

"You know that I have disposed of my family business interests, and have little influence in these matters."

"Ah, Don Benito, my hope was that you might take the poor, frightened child under your wing, so to speak. Surely that would forestall anyone's action against her, would it not?"

Escalara laughed out loud. "You see, Emilio, how it is with these Celts? The Irish, especially. My friend Terrence, that still would leave your Mr. Cathcart out on the proverbial limb, would it not?"

"It has occurred to me that perhaps, if it were rumored that he had deliberately procured the girl for you, it might deter what would otherwise be certain retribution."

"'Certain retribution,' is it? Is this not one Celt trying to save another from his just rewards?"

"I never thought of that, your honor, but now that you mention it..."

"Terrence Riordan, you have brightened an old man's day. I make no promise, and certainly if we can make this happen your friend will be out his ten thousand, but let us see what we can do." Don Benito considered a moment longer as Riordan murmured his thanks. "Terrence, an associate of mine operates a charter/lease business from the El Paso Airport. I am writing his name and number on the back of this card. You might give him a call; who knows, he might need a pilot with the gift of the Irish."

Don Benito turned serious for a second: "One more thing. Your Mr. Clay has a friend, a Mr. Stensvahl, if I am not mistaken."

"I don't know that they are exactly friends, but he does know him," Riordan answered cautiously.

"Perhaps he would be well advised to keep some distance from Stensvahl."

After Cap'n Eddie took his leave, Escalara turned to his companion and said, "Well, my friend, we have had our entertainment from the day, have we not? Mr. Shakespeare was indeed correct when he referred to all the world being a stage..."

Terrence "Cap'n Eddie" Riordan shivered involuntarily when he walked back across the border to the customs shed and the door marked 'Pedestrians/ Peotones.' The phrase, *life is never simple* fluttered at the edge of his mind. He presented his passport which was duly scrutinized by the customs agent, who, in violation of all unwritten rules, actually smiled at him for a second or two. He crossed the highway to the car park barely noticing the campesino soliciting a northbound ride, entered his car and sped off to his quarters, six miles away. The first thing he did after he arrived was to pour a stiff scotch, the second was to drink it.

Thelma and Thurman

They sat at the small patio table that held a bottle containing perhaps another half glass apiece of wine. She had let her hair grow down to almost to her shoulders; it was shimmering in the gathering dusk. New Mexico was favoring them with another of her breathtaking sunsets. Dark purple clouds had gathered above the horizon and scattered on to the east from there. The western rim of each formation was a fiery gold that tinged orange-crimson before meeting the main velvety lavender/purple mass. The sun itself still hung on the shoulder of the Tres Hermana's South Peak, a brilliant silver disc. John Henry Clay sipped his wine, at peace with the world and seemingly at peace with himself.

Wanda was bird watching. Two curved-bill thrashers were working feverishly to rebuild an old nest in a cholla about 20 feet from where they sat. "They're using mesquite twigs," she observed.

"Yeah. About every third one will fall out as they stomp around in there. They are working on the penthouse."

"But they work so hard at it. How long have they been nest building?"

"They've been goin' at it about three years now, off and on, I believe. By the way, that's Thelma and Thurman you're watching."

"Really." She sounded incredulous but willing to give him the benefit of doubt.

"John Henry, I wouldn't take you for a birder."

"I'm not. I don't keep anything like a Life List, I just enjoy watching them. Those two work their asses off rebuilding but I think they have only seen one chick make it beyond fledging. It's kind of like the world in a microcosm."

"Why you old fart," she said with no little affection, "you do have a romantic streak. Who'd have thought it?" She laid her hand on his across the table.

"Damn! The secret's out."

They spent a quiet few minutes before she spoke again. "So, John Henry, how is your little protégé doing?"

"Ah... well, the season's about over, they've washed out of the tournament... she's looking for a summer job and another boyfriend, since she dumped the old one. She has her father's talent, I think, and certainly her mother's height. She'll do well, I hope."

"Her mother's height? Her dad's the tall one. Didn't you say he was six-six or so?"

"Well, yes, but the coaches tell me that what really counts is how tall mom is. According to Denny Aye, he always wanted to meet mother first, 'cause he could see how tall she was – though most of all because it was mom who engineered where the kid would end up in college."

"She is college material? I mean, is she smart enough as well as good enough?"

Well, she's like a lot of kids, 'A' in the subjects she likes, 'C' in the others. No, she has enough talent that someone in the Big Twelve or even the ACC will snap her up."

"John Henry?"

"Yeah?"

"For a real asshole, you're a pretty nice guy."

"Wow. Terms of endearment."

Day 6

The Meeting

Eddie turned off the TV where he had been watching Headline News. "Lollipop news," he exclaimed in disgust. He retrieved his clothing from the dryer and took the basket back into the living room of the singlewide. John Henry was in the process of searing the small pieces of pork needed in preparing green chili stew for their supper. "You still planning to head out tomorrow?'

Eddie looked up from folding his clothing. "I've been mooching off you for long enough. The Res calls, you know how it is..."

Clay's phone rang and he answered, "Hello?"

"Mr. Clay?"

"Yes it is."

"Mr. Clay, I am calling you in reference to the materials Tomas wanted to discuss."

"Yes?"

"I have the hope that we might be able to meet and exchange information."

"Hold on a second please," Clay covered the mouthpiece and motioned to Eddie Sam. He then switched the phone to speaker. "Go ahead."

"Mr. Clay, is it possible for us to meet?"

"It might be; what do you have in mind?"

"I arrive in El Paso tomorrow about 9:30 in the morning. You are on Mountain Time, no?"

"Mountain Daylight, yes."

"I can be in Columbus by noon. If you are not busy, we

can meet at a place of your choosing. I would, however, like to keep our meeting somewhat private if we can."

"Alright. I am assuming you will take Highway 9, the border road from El Paso. As you start down off the caprock, or mesa, you will see Columbus for the first time. It is about 15 miles off at that point. A third of the way down the grade, there is a pull-off, a car park. I will be there promptly at noon. By the way, do you have a name?"

"I will be there. Just call me Pablo," and he hung up.

Eddie looked up at John Henry, "Good English, spoken like a Columbian. You want backup on this one? It won't hurt any if I don't get away tomorrow."

"You think I need it?"

Eddie turned as serious as John Henry had ever seen him. "Look, Mikos goes out of his way to put you on alert. This Tomas spills everything he knows, including your name to the bad guys. They don't know what your involvement is, but, then they don't care, they just want to cover all bases. You don't have the slightest what your buddy Dub has been up to, only that you know he's pissed off a fair amount of the citizenry along the border. Do you need backup? Oh, hell, I don't know, waddya think?"

"Since you put it that way, oh golden tongue..."

"OK, so we will do this one by the book. We are going to pretend we once operated in the field and that we know how to avoid being set up. That alright with you?"

Grudgingly, John Henry said, "Yeah."

"You gonna check this out with Mikos?"

"Yeah, but let's eat dinner first."

The two of them left Clay's house shortly after 11 AM, turned off Missouri Street onto the border road, New Mexico 9, and headed east. As they passed the site of the 1916 First Aero Squadron Aerodrome, Eddie Sam turned slightly from the drivers seat and said to his passenger, "Unless this guy is lying to you, the only way he can get here within his time frame is to come through Santa Teresa on this road. Ain't another way, period."

"Your point is?"

"I'm just saying. You know, tradecraft."

"Bullshit."

For about 14 miles the asphalt two-lane ran straight as an arrow across 76 Draw until it reached the base of the bluff where a siding called 'Arena' once stood. The only remnant was a windmill and a corral. The road hooked to the left and began the ascent to the broad mesa, or caprock, that separated the flats where Columbus and Palomas stood from the Rio Grande Valley and El Paso, some 50 miles distant. Passing the proposed meeting place on the left (and noting that it was empty), the two continued at a leisurely pace almost to the county line where Sam pulled up, did a three point turn on the empty highway, and pulled on to the berm. They sat there, counting west bound vehicles for about 20 minutes before a Border Patrol Jeep pulled in behind them.

"Morning, gentlemen," he said, "You folks having a problem?"

"Good morning. No sir, we are just killing time. We are to meet a fella over on the grade and we are a bit early."

"You both US Citizens?"

A chorus, "Yessir."

"You mind if I look through your vehicle?"

Since it was Clay's truck, Eddie looked over at him; Clay nodded his assent. "Eddie, you wanna open the hatch on the topper? I'll get the third door."

When Clay joined the other two at the rear of the truck, the BPO Agent was examining the contents, a mattress elevated about a foot between the fender wells. Holding the mattress off the floor were two aluminum deep drawer units, which John Henry opened for the Agent. "I use this thing as a camper," he explained.

The Border Patrol drove off without further comment. Eddie noted, "You watch, he'll be eyeballing us like a hawk from out there in the bush someplace."

At two minutes before the hour, they pulled into the car park. There was a new black Suburban parked there, close to the edge of the lot. Eddie stopped about 10 meters away. "Did he pass us when that BP had us out of the truck? I don't re-member it, do you?"

Clay's only comment was, "Interesting." He stepped from the pickup, walked close to the Suburban's drivers side, and asked, "Pablo?"

"Yes. Please get in."

Clay walked around the front of the SUV, reached out to the hood as if to steady himself as he walked, and got into the passenger seat. The hood was warm, not hot.

Pablo smiled thinly. He seemed average height, Hispan-ic and dressed expensively city-casual in slacks, polo shirt and light weight sport jacket. Clay noticed that he wore a signet on his left hand and Rolex on his right wrist. It was not hard to imagine him as an agent of some sort.

"I see you believe in caution, Mr. Clay. In our business it is always wise."

"Just what is our business, sir?"

"Ah, Mr. Clay, you know we are here to discuss Mr. Dub Stensvahl."

"I am a trifle dubious, sir. Frankly, I find it hard to swal-low that you would waste the time or the money to travel here to interview someone that barely knows Stensvahl."

"I am here because I could tie other business into this meeting. Mr. Stensvahl at one time was the center of a money transfer operation. When the war broke out down here, Don Benito's father gave a fairly large sum to him with the idea that he would reestablish himself somewhere else. He only stayed away until the old man died, then came back, but none of the factions, other than perhaps the Death Angels, would even talk to him. Because of his knowledge, he suddenly became a liability. The government would very much like to chat with him. I have been given to understand that his present grasp of reality is weak at best. Is this true?"

"I don't know that I could speak to that. His behavior in the mountains last fall didn't seem too stable; but I haven't been face-to-face with the man for quite some time."

"I see." Whether Pablo saw or not, John Henry wasn't sure. "Mr. Clay – may I call you John Henry? We are interested in what Stensvahl might lead us to now as well as in the future. I do not wish to frighten him off because he could be a very valuable witness for us. Perhaps we need to be working through an intermediary?"

Oh ho, I see where you are going. Who can you get to set him up... not I, said the Little Red Hen. "Nobody that I know of is close enough to him to make any difference."

"Not even you, John Henry Clay? I have heard that he trusts you. Goodness knows, you seem to have been completely reimbursed for his original insult."

I'll be damned. How does he know that? Walk easy, John Henry. "Pablo, if he is as paranoid as I think he is, you won't get within a hundred feet without spooking him."

"Ah... do you think that would be true of his daughter, also?"

"I believe that there are several folks who might take real exception to someone trying to use the daughter. Might want to tread easy, there."

The small smile again. "John Henry, if you were to approach him, how do you think would be the best way to do it?"

"I'm told he is a mortgage broker in Scottsdale now. I'd just make an appointment with him to talk finance. Meeting him on his home ground might be the best way to do it; I don't know."

They chatted about nothing of substance for another minute or two before Clay said good-bye. He walked slowly back to his truck. "Do we follow him?" Eddie asked.

"Why? He wouldn't do anything but run us in circles."

"I knew that."

Day 7

Agnes Two Pony

She pulled the old Chevy into a parking spot, shifted the transmission to P, turned the key to the off position and sat there for a moment. The feeling of disquiet that had plagued her all morning would not go away. She had volunteered to do her sister's shopping in Silver City, but decided to detour via the Mimbres Ranger Station. Jose Ortega was behind the counter, playing Spider on the computer. He looked away from his game, "Oh, hello, Agnes. What's up?"

"Your time, buddy, your time when I rat you out to Wanda. Is she around?"

"Naw. Right about now she ought to be in Hillsboro, I think. Meeting with the water district people."

"She hear anything more about her job? Hell, she's been 'Acting Chief' going on forever now."

"Be serious. She's not gonna get the job. They are promoting women now, but she has two or three guys in front of her that have to die before she gets the full appointment. Same ol', same ol'."

"You ever hear anything about the Reverend Orville Foss? Is he still up in the woods making idiots of you guys?"

"Hey, not me. I don't care if they get him or not, and I'm willing to bet the Feds don't care much, either."

"If Wanda doesn't get the permanent job, what'll she do?"

"Oh, she'll go back to Enforcement. She spent most of her time over there. If she keeps her head down she can probably pick some plum before she retires. Helluva lot better than I'm gonna do."

Scottsdale

Julie Stensvahl had a highly successful sophomore season, in spite of her team not making it to the state finals. A Las Cruces sports writer noted that she had been working on her left hand and was really hustling for rebounds. He predicted a bright future for her. Clay had taken to attending most of her home games and even the occasional away contest. She, in turn, had, from time to time, invested small confidences in the big man and he would have been the first to admit that his ego was bolstered by it.

Dub Stensvahl had made the transition to a full days work at First Valley Mortgage without a great deal of difficulty. They had given him a lot of freedom and not asked too many questions. He was a good salesman and a good producer who understood finance; what more could you ask? At 10:35, Stensvahl asked Mrs. McCumber, the group secretary, for a donut and cup of coffee. Back at his computer, he brought up the El Paso Times and keyed the current news icon. He scanned the financial news for a while. In the course of his reading, Dub brought up a sidebar headed "Local Violence." He was about to abandon it when his eye caught the word "banker" followed the name "Perez-Lopez." Sr. Perez had been kidnapped the week previous, the article reported, then found mutilated in the desert south of Santa Teresa, an El Paso suburb.

He sat there for several minutes, staring out the window but seeing nothing. Finally, Stensvahl shut down the computer, slipped into his navy blazer, and told the secretary that he needed to run home for a bit but would probably be back after lunch. She thought no more about it, nor did she take notice that the afternoon did not produce Dub Stensvahl again.

He left the office via the rear freight dock, circled the block so as to come to the parking garage from the opposite direction and carefully scanned the street before he sought out his car. He had leased a BMW 740Li, and the thousand a month payment was killing him, but he reasoned that he had to keep up appearances, even if it meant sleeping in the back seat. In truth, he loved the car. It had all the bells and whistles, including a remote start feature.

He slipped into the three story car park, took the steps to the second floor and again ascertained that he was alone before actually leaving the stairwell. Dub located his Beemer halfway down the parking level and approached it carefully. He stopped about four cars distant and sheltering behind a concrete pillar, pressed the remote start button. The car started almost instantly, purring softly in the shade of the deck above it. He counted one thousand-one to one thousand-sixty before walking to the car, opening the door and getting in. He backed out of the parking slot, shifted to 'D' and pulled smoothly out of the building.

He headed down the 101 to Tempe and his rented storage cell where he loaded all his outdoor gear and spare clothing into the car. He drove in circles for a bit, trying to decide whether he was being followed. Finally leaving the Phoenix area, he drove south on I-10 directly to the Tucson Airport and pulled into the long-term parking area where he found a slot next to an older red Ford Ranger truck. He entered the terminal and bought a ticket to Las Vegas, charging it to his American Express card, then returned to the car to decide what his next steps should be.

By 10:30 the next morning, Mrs. McCumber had spent several minutes trying to decide whether she should call Mr. Oesper, her boss, to report the missing Dub Stensvahl. She decided against it, and called the number Dub had listed in his personnel file again. That produced only a recording saying that the owner of the phone "...was not taking calls at that time, but if the caller would..." and Mrs. McCumber hung up. Dub had only two appointments scheduled and she could easily route those to other staff.

Day 8

Walkabout Again

The call Clay attempted to Mikos went unreturned. Eddie had unpacked. He decided to stick around a while if only to watch John Henry's back. Watch it from what, neither knew. From past training, they knew that the best way to handle the situation was to stay out in the open among as many people as they could during the day; and to go undercover at night into the safest quarters they could arrange. Their collective thinking was that because he didn't appear to be a principal player in the ongoing drama, it would be that whoever was gunning for John Henry, if that were indeed the case, would be unlikely to try for Clay on this side of the border, at least during the day. So, no change in daily routine, except maybe, just maybe, a little more peeking back over the shoulder.

They ate a quiet breakfast at El Portal, kibitzing with Joe Ramirez and two other customs agents they didn't know. They walked across the street to the Columbus Library where Eddie picked up his e-mail in their computer room, reputedly second in size only to Santa Fe and Albuquerque. For a while they passed the time of day with Charles Rosen, one of the village trustees (and the only one not related to Hizzonor). They took some time to look over the latest display of art there, before walking catty-corner across Broadway to the Main (and only) Post Office, where Clay collected his mail and schmoozed with three or four other citizens bent on the same task.

Clay and Sam walked back down Broadway to what passed for the offices of Frontera Tours, John Henry's sometime employer. April was seated at her desk behind a copy of the El Paso Times.

John Henry Clay had sprawled his six feet, eight and a fraction inch frame in the only comfortable chair owned by Frontera Tours while Eddie had propped himself in a settee on the opposite wall.

"Hello, beautiful," chimed Eddie Sam.

"Go to hell, Eddie," was the reply.

"What?"

"You know damn good and well, 'what'," she said.

"I know when I'm not wanted."

"Your perception is better than your judgment," she said.

Now it was Clay's turn, "What?"

"Oh, I did my best to fix her up with a date, and this is the thanks I get. No good deed goes unpunished."

John Henry sighed dramatically, "I know there is a fascinating story here, but I'll wait if it's just the same to you all."

April said, "J.H., some guy just tried to call you. Wouldn't leave his name, so I didn't volunteer anything. Said he'd already tried you at home, but he'd try again later. Look, you two, I have been trying to get ahold of you for almost a week. Can't you check in once in a while?"

"April, are we working this week?"

"Not so far. I have you set up for a week Wednesday for a daytrip to Mata Ortiz. Some late snowbirds, I think. That gonna be alright?"

"Yeah, unless Poochie can think up a reason to put me in the slammer."

"I think you're safe. He took off for Santa Fe this morning with Hizzonor. Begging at the Governor's table again, I suppose."

April looked at John Henry, then at Eddie Sam. "Let's get back to something. I have been meaning to talk to you both and as long as you're here..." *Oh-oh, this is serious,* John Henry thought. *But, then, April is always serious...* He began an examination of his fingernails.

"The two of you are dinosaurs. Look at you. You are electronic delinquents. You don't have a computer between you, but that doesn't matter because you are barely computer literate. You don't know what a blackberry is, let alone own one. You don't tweet, I can't find either of you on Face Book, you don't even carry a cell with you every day. J.H., I know you have a GPS and I also know that you leave it in your pack most of the time. How am I supposed to run a business without being able to keep in contact with at least one of you guys. Am I right? You know damn good and well I am!"

"Aw, lay off, April," Eddie Sam said. He was ignored. He continued anyhow, "Look, we're just a couple of guys trying to get along on what we got. A few brains and a little skill. We aren't technos and we never will be. Take us for what we are – a couple workin' stiffs, just doin' what we can do."

April turned back to Clay, sighing, "J.H., you could at least have the courtesy to check in once in a while – at least to let me know you're back in town." April was the only one he knew that called him by his initials.

"Yes, Ma'am."

"Don't you give me that 'yes Ma'am' crap, either. I know you like a book, John Henry, and I know when you are being patronizing."

"Yes, Ma'am, I'm sorry. I was dead tired when I got in last night and I slept in this morning. It's my fault completely. And I didn't mean to sound patronizing."

Her anger finally dissipated, April abandoned the subject, having done as much as she could with it considering the two louts involved. She sighed again.

They had been back at the singlewide for about 45 minutes when the phone rang. "This'll be your mysterious call," Eddie said.

Clay shrugged, picked up the phone. "Hello."

"Mr. Clay, this is Pablo. Your friend has skipped again. Any ideas?"

"None. How do you know this?" he knew the question was unnecessary.

"I just thought I would check with you to see if you had any inkling of where he would go."

"I told you, no"

"How about Las Vegas?"

"Pablo, I do not have a clue. Not a clue. He could have gone back to the Mimbres; he could have gone to Wichita for all I know."

"Why would he go to Wichita?"

"I don't know that he would. I just used that as an example."

"I see. Thank you, Mr. Clay." He hung up.

About 11 AM they left for the 30 mile drive to the Deming Walmart to stock up on groceries and for Eddie to pick up some more underwear.

Clay had two calls early the next morning. The first was from Pablo, the second from a distraught ex-Mrs. Dub Stensvahl.

Pablo wanted to enlarge on their conversation of the day before, but this time his focus was on John Henry's mention of the Mimbres Wilderness. What the 10 minute conversation boiled down to was this: would Clay be willing to guide Pablo to where Dub might be hiding? When John Henry declined, a shade less than politely, Pablo said, "Please think it over Mr. Clay. We know that he tried to lay a false trail for us; we know that he has hidden there in the past. We might be yet able to save him from himself. Please, I will leave you a number, call me back if you change your mind."

As he switched off the phone, he said to Eddie Sam, "He seems convinced Dub's gone back to the Mimbres. If I don't guide him in, there are a half-dozen others who will, all he has to do is make a couple calls. I don't want any part of it."

Not quite a half hour later Dianne Stensvahl called. The thrust of her call was simple: Julie had left home without word as to where she was headed. Her latest boyfriend had driven her and her hiking gear onto the Lake Road and dropped her near the Ruby Creek-Weber Creek confluence where she had sworn him to silence. Fortunately, his silence did not last longer than a confrontation with his mother who had immediately called Dianne.

"You're gonna go, right?"

"Eddie, I'm not sure. If Dub's up there..."

"I don't know what difference it makes. If he's up there,

we can still get her out. If they go into hiding, between the two of us, we ought to be able to find them; we are supposed to be trackers."

"And if she doesn't want to come? Do we drag her out?"

"Yeah, I see what you mean... John Henry, what about this? We take that Pablo character into the Mimbres with us. Let him deal with Dub and at the same time let the girl see all the circumstances."

"What you mean, 'we', Kemo Sabe?"

"Come on, man. You surely wouldn't go in there alone with him, would you? We think he's alright, but we don't know that. I'd like to hear from Mikos in any case."

"Eddie, it is going to be bad enough if two of us go barging into that canyon. Three of us would seem like an army... it'd scare them off for sure. Besides, if this guy is a bad actor, you know damn well I can lose him in a flash."

"Not if he has the drop on you... or for that matter, leaves you beside the trail with a bullet in you."

"Without me, he'd never find them."

"Don't bet your life on that. I'm thinking that you will pick up their sign before you get up the trail a hundred feet – if they are there. Once you are on the trail up the mountain you will pointing him right at them."

John Henry mulled that one over. "OK, let's go back to basics. What are we trying to do here? First, we want Julie clear of any nastiness. Second, as good citizens aren't we trying to connect Dub with the Feds?"

"Good citizens, my ass. Leave Stensvahl there to rot as far as I'm concerned. Just get the girl out."

In the end they reached a compromise. John Henry would guide Pablo to Dub, if Dub were indeed there. Eddie Sam would back him up as closely as he could without being seen. He would give Clay a half hour to an hour head start, but John Henry had to promise he wouldn't push the pace too hard so that Sam could keep up without difficulty, unseen. John Henry called Pablo and made the necessary arrangements. He did not tell him about Julie.

Day 9

To the Mimbres

Pablo was waiting in front of the library with his gear. When Clay pulled up, he loaded his pack into John Henry's pickup, then mounted the cab beside him. Watching from across the street in front of El Portal were Archie Miles and Cap'n Eddie Riordan, just leaving a late breakfast. Cap'n Eddie studied the figures in the truck until they turned right on Highway 11 and vanished from sight. Something bothered him; where had he seen that guy before? Before he could work it out, Miles had asked him what he was up to today. Cap'n Eddie replied, "Well, I gotta get to the airport by two to report for work." It then came to him where he had seen the man in question.

Eddie Sam had rather unceremoniously dumped his back-country gear in the rear of his jeep, turned out the lights and was starting out of the door when a rental Dodge stopped in front of the mobile home. The man who emerged was 6'1" or so, well dressed, slightly on the stocky side, probably Mexican, and seemed in a hurry.

When he assured him he was not John Henry Clay, but Eddie Sam, the man seemed perplexed for a moment. Then his face brightened, "You are Mr. Clay's tracker friend, right?" The English was impeccable. Eddie assured him that he was.

"Mr. Sam, allow me to introduce myself. I am Coronel Esteban Morales of the Republic of Mexico's Federal Justice Police," and he produced an ID card from a document folder.

Damn. The Federales. "El Coronel, how may I be of service?"

"Mr. Sam, we, in cooperation with elements of your

Federal Government, have been investigating an affair involving a Mr. Dub Stensvahl."

Oh, shit.

"I am afraid a known assassin, one Andres Prieto, is stalking Stensvahl, and he seems to be in contact with your friend Clay."

Pedro? Pablo?- whatever the hell his name is.

Nothing ventured... Eddie Sam invited the man in and sat him at the table. He again examined the proffered credentials. *"Mi Coronel,* we may have a problem," and he then explained the situation in some detail.

Morales at first seemed taken aback when Eddie finished. After a few seconds, he said, "Mr. Sam, it seems to me that we must waste no time in catching up to your friend. I am sure this Pablo is none other than the assassin Prieto; he will simply kill all who are involved as he thinks he needs to. We must do this, and must hurry. I need to pick up one man who will be of assistance and then we must go."

My better judgment tells me not to do this, but...

Eddie made the necessary arrangements to meet Morales after El Coronel picked up his gear and his man. When Morales took his leave, he left Eddie slightly puzzled. For one thing Sam felt he needed to create some kind of backup for this new plan, just in case...

First, he tried Clay's cell without success. *He could be in any one of a dozen dead zones.*

Next, Sam punched in the number Clay had entered for Agnes Two Pony into his land line. Her sister answered on the fourth ring. She spoke little English, and Eddie's Navajo was rusty, but he managed to convey the need for Agnes to call him back. Satisfied that he had done what he could under the circumstances, he mounted his Jeep and drove off. Shortly after he left, the phone on Clay's counter rang. It was answered by the voice mail recording, and the caller said, "This is Mikos..."

He and Morales were to meet at the old Sunshine School, about halfway to Deming. Eddie waited just short of twenty minutes before the Federales made their appearance. When they arrived, it was in an enormous Hummer, licensed in New

Mexico, Sam noted. Morales was riding in the second row seating, and was insistent that the three of them ride together, Eddie in the rear with him. This arrangement, of course, meant leaving Eddie's Jeep behind. The man driving interested Sam, if for no other reason than he was obviously a Tarahumara Indian, and he could not remember ever seeing a Tarahumara on the US side of the line.

Sam remembered a few Tarahumara words, including their greeting. *"Cuira,"* he said. The Indian looked slightly startled, but said nothing. He was dressed in clean, well worn jeans, white Guyabarra shirt. He was slender to the point of being almost emaciated; Eddie guessed his age at between 40 and 50. Morales did not introduce them.

Unlike the Navajo and a number of other tribes who simply described themselves as "the People" (Dine in Navajo), the Tarahumara referred to themselves as "Raramura," *the runners*. They were, in fact, second only to Eddie Sam's own tribe in North American Indian population, something Eddie had gleaned during a short sojourn in Mexico's Copper Canyon. He knew they were prodigious runners and could be prodigious drinkers as well. His only recent exposure was to the many plump Tarahumara women in traditional dress who begged in the streets of Palomas. He had been told that while their men accompanied the women to border towns and the women begged, the husbands stayed largely out of sight.

In many ways the Tarahumara were throwbacks to another era. As the Spanish civilization encroached on their homelands in Mexico, they retreated further and further into the rugged mountains of the Sierra Madre Ocidental. They remained settled in the far reaches of the Copper Canyon in the State of Sinaloa. The Copper Canyon, *Barranca del Cobre,* was actually a series of canyons deeper and far, far broader than our own Grand Canyon. While most spoke at least some Spanish, Tarahumara remained their first language, especially among the women. They eked out a living herding goats on tiny *ranchitos* and many migrated to the cities from time to time to beg.

Eddie was even more puzzled by the attitude of Morales

toward the Indian. He was certainly condescending, berating the Tarahumara for holding them up, for not packing the right gear and, it seemed, for just being alive. Morales referred to him as 'Ignacio'; apparently the Tarahumara spoke only broken Spanish, and Eddie surmised, no English at all. "Los Indios!" Morales spat out. Eddie wondered if that included himself as well.

They picked up Highway 180 just north of Deming. Near the Duke Power Plant, Eddie's cell phone rang. *"Ya-ta-hay,"* he greeted in Navajo. Agnes Two Pony Replied in kind.

He continued in Navaho: "Agnes, stay with speaking Dine. Tell me a story, I will explain as we talk." He put his hand over the transmitter in such a way that he hoped Agnes could overhear. "My mother's sister. Speaks only Navajo. Her husband is drunk again," he explained.

"Eddie Sam, you are a worthless peckerhead. You must be the one that's drunk."

"Agnes," he cajoled, "play along with me. The Big Guy may be in deep *guano*." Both the Ignacio and Morales understood 'guano' and smiled.

"Well, I could tell you the story of my life..." and she continued in that vein, sounding vaguely angry, with Eddie nodding from time to time. At one point he turned to Morales and shrugged, seeming to say, "What can I do?"

Finally, Eddie broke in and in short bursts, explained that while he had hoped to watch Clay's back, he was now a couple hours behind schedule. "I don't know what you can do, but you are at least an hour closer to him than I am," he concluded. Agnes rang off.

Morales asked, "Everything straightened out?"

Eddie shrugged, said, "Do these things ever get straightened out?" That elicited a chuckle from the Federale.

Agnes replaced the phone in its cradle. She was confused, Eddie was obviously in some sort of situation that he could not explain in the open. John Henry was in a situation where he was at risk from the man with whom he was travelling. Everyone was headed into the Mimbres Wilderness, back to the No-Name Creek canyon. She consulted her watch, and decided that Eddie Sam and party could not make it up the mountain to the canyon before dark; in fact, might be stopped far short of it. She could be on the trail well before Sam and if she hustled, might almost catch up to Clay and his companion. But what if she did? Then what? As the man once said, it was a puzzlement.

She told her brother-in-law that she needed a ride to the Mimbres Ranger Station – NOW.

Agnes was carrying her pack out to his truck when she stopped dead in her tracks, considered for a moment, then called out to him. They conferred for some thirty seconds; her brother-in-law broke away shaking his head, but returned several minutes later carrying a Walmart bag that contained something fairly heavy from the look of it. They got in the truck together and left in a cloud of dust.

Hot on the Trail

Eddie Sam had been right. Clay found the girl's footprints almost right away, before they had gone several hundred meters. He still had not mentioned her to Pablo; he didn't know why. He was actually looking for some sign of Dub, but they needed to cover ground because of the late start so he wasn't actually tracking. He spent about 10 minutes at the point Black Run intersected Weber Creek, again seeing Julie's track but no sign of Dub. By itself, he knew that it might mean only that Stensvahl was being careful. Pablo seemed to be fairly well equipped, although he didn't seem to be carrying a tent. *If it rains – and it might – he'll wish he had one.* By the time they approached Gooseberry Canyon, Pablo was lagging, breathing hard. He was obviously not a quitter or complainer, but he just wasn't in very good shape, Clay decided. He called a halt and produced a couple trail bars. Pablo seemed happy for the break and asked, "How much farther now?"

"Too far to make tonight, I think. See the canyon just ahead? That has a couple of old rockfalls that we will have to scramble, lose some time there. We'll cut us a couple of walking sticks before we go in, that'll help. But we'll have to pitch camp at the base of the final trail climb, in a place they call Cienaga. It is not really a bog, just a big seep about this time of year. We'll make fire and have a decent meal; then get out early and climb it tomorrow."

Pablo didn't offer a reply.

When Eddie Sam and party arrived at the trailhead they parked between Clay's pickup and two other vehicles, an old Volvo and a red Ford Ranger. Eddie stretched and did some limbering exercises while Ignacio unloaded. When they stepped from the Hummer Edie noticed that the Indian was wearing only *hueraches* on his feet, the ubiquitous peasant sandals.

As Sam shouldered his pack, he also noticed that Morales donned what looked like a small day-pack, and the Tarahumara shrugged into a pack that made Sam's look paltry. *What is going on here?* he wondered. As if reading his thoughts, Morales informed him that Ignacio's primary function was as a bearer, something the Tarahumara were good at, he seemed to admit grudgingly. Still, Morales spent a good bit of trail time bitching about, or at, Ignacio. The Indian did not answer him or even change his expression.

Gooseberry Canyon Again

Clay recalled that the canyon passage was not an easy one to begin with, but snowmelt had brought down more debris at the two scrambles and the volume of water trying to make it through those rockfalls had dramatically increased. Water surged from a dozen places near the top of the blockage and seemed to squirt from hundreds of other places in the rock fall. Unlike the second barrier Clay knew they would encounter, this one stepped up irregularly from the creek bed which itself was now considerably wider and deeper than he recalled. While this first one was more a true scramble than a climb, nonetheless the ascent proved to be much more difficult than when Clay had ascended in the fall, partly due to Pablo's seeming inexperience and partly due to the need to fight through the surging water.

Pablo was near exhaustion by the time they reached the second barrier. He suggested that they make camp here instead of pressing on, but John Henry would hear none of it. "Man, the way this creek is running now it would not take much of a storm to turn this canyon into a death trap. Look how narrow it is – almost a slot canyon. Where would we run to?"

"We could use one of those ledges," Pablo said, pointing to one about 5 meters over their heads.

"Pablo, do you see those striations – scrapes – along the wall, off to the left and up about five or six meters? No, there a little further left, up above that ledge. Yeah. Those were put there debris carried by a flood. Where do you figure we'd be if something like that came through again?"

Izzy Garza hunkered down against a house-sized boulder, high on the ridge overlooking Forest Trail 805. He had begun to observe the pair of Harris' hawks about a week ago and had finally located their nest the day before in an old and partially dead ponderosa pine not far from Weber Creek. He had been finishing his work as early as he could when he was in the area in order to keep an eye on the birds. While their nesting habitat seemed right, the locale seemed fairly far from their hunting area and his curiosity was aroused.

He had already observed recent tracks heading off toward Gooseberry Canyon and his interest was piqued when his binoculars revealed John Henry Clay, followed closely by a smaller man arriving on FT 805 and then taking the turnoff along Black Run. An hour or so later, Agnes Two Pony followed the same route. Izzy was just about to pack it in for the day when Eddie Sam and party passed him by. Something, Izzy decided, is up. *It looks like a goddam convention*, he thought. Never a man to rush at a task, he considered things for a while, then made up his mind. Climbing to a position where he knew the Ranger Station could receive his radio signal, he reported the goings-on to Jose Ortega, who in turn told Wanda Brubaker.

Wanda was decidedly not happy. There had been no back country requests for over a week. Wanda walked out to the radio, ordered Izzy to follow the last bunch at a discreet distance, and told him she would catch up to him sometime in the morning. At that point, cooler thinking took over and she said, "Izzy, do you have overnight gear with you?"

"No, ma'am, I don't."

"OK, then, here's what we do: be ready to roll first thing in the morning. I'll meet you at the trailhead at first light, and then we'll go see just what's going on."

"10-4."

Had Izzy gone ahead and done what Ranger Brubaker had first ordered him to do, he would have intercepted a Tarahumara in full pack loping down FT 805 toward the trailhead. Or, if he had taken his time leaving the Wilderness, the Indian might have overtaken him. As it was, neither took place. Izzy hurried home to pack and Ignacio left the Mimbres unnoticed.

Even later, after Eddie Sam had some time to think about what happened, it was a blur. Ignacio, Col. Morales and he had made it to the first scramble in Gooseberry without a great deal of difficulty. The Indian had carried his own load as well as most of Morales' without complaint. The Federale, for his part had hiked without lagging too badly, although Eddie knew they could have made better time had he been willing to push a little. Morales kept a running commentary going about the Frontera, Mexican and US politics, the Army and the Border Patrol, none of which he was particularly enthralled with. As he expounded however, he worked in derogatory comments about the aptitude of the Tarahumara in general, the condition of Ignacio's hometown of Sinforosa, and the demeanor of Ignacio in particular. Ignacio said nothing, his expression never changing. Eddie's attempts to end the monolog or to change the topics met with no success.

On entering Gooseberry Canyon, Sam had cut walking staves for each of them, making sure they were sturdy enough to support a good deal of weight on the climbs, and long enough to use for pushing off. The first barrier was mostly stepped, a combination scramble and climb as Clay had noted. The Tarahumara seemed to have little difficulty in spite of his pack and his footgear. Sam went up last, figuring to assist Morales, who declined his help. Eddie did observe, however, that the climb seemed to deplete the last of the Federale's energy. Both he and the officer were fairly soaked as they resumed the hike, picking their way through the boulders and the water, Morales had little to say.

The second rockfall presented them with a real challenge. The barrier was only about 12 feet or so high, but it was almost vertical. Eddie and Ignacio discussed the technique to be used, Sam recalling that Clay had climbed it first then pulled his pack up after him. The Tarahumara nodded in assent, and said, "I will go first. Maybe you next, we put a rope on El Coronel, and we will help him that way?"

Eddie nodded. "OK, but we send the packs up after you, then I come up."

Ignacio nodded, slipped out of his pack and, picking what looked like the easiest way, started his climb. He was within a few feet of the top when he stopped, backed down several feet, stopped again and considered before moving to another route. This apparently worked for him, since he was able to push himself over the top several feet to the north of where he originally attempted.

Eddie stood and applauded. "Excelente! Nice job!" Morales said nothing.

Eddie had studied Ignacio's climb, trying to remember exactly where he placed his feet. Then he had the Tarahumara toss all their cordage back to him as soon as they had the packs on the top of the scramble. When Eddie tied enough together to make a double pull rope, he made a rough saddle by tying a double bowline on a bight. He turned to Morales and instructed him on its use.

"Do not put your full weight on the rope, it may not hold. We will use it to steady you, and to give you a little extra lift when you need it. It will be entirely up to you to keep yourself on the wall."

With a little help from Ignacio, Eddie's ascent was without problems. Next, they needed to bring up the Mexican officer.

Déjà vu

John Henry Clay almost didn't recognize it. Much of the Cienaga had turned from November's trickles to broad ribbons of shallow water, and where there was not actually running water the sand was wet and spongy. *Keep your eye out for quicksand,* he thought. *The sheer magic of water.* No-Name Creek had all but disappeared; the embankment over which it fell in late fall now glistened in the fading sun from the far end of the notch on the south to the small landslip at the north – perhaps 150 meters worth – small cascades of water seeping from within the mountain side. Tiny yellow flowers (mallows?) carpeted the embanked area. Tiny ferns prospered in odd places. Several small pools at the base of the embankment gathered the flow and fed Black Run. The game trail he originally climbed still skirted most of the wet as it made its way up the slope, switching back and forth over the thin creek bed. Although ponderosa pine dominated the hillsides mixed with a scattering of pinon, on the cutbank around the north side of the Cienaga several small willows vied for space with a few boxelder. Adding to the confusion of growth were chokecherries in full bloom, alive with bees. He had no doubt that the *tinaja* that formed the source of No-Name Creek was bursting with water. Here in the high country, a joyous spring was in full engagement.

John Henry and Pablo had made camp opposite the seeping wall. Clay observed that his companion was no stranger to camp life as they put a fire together and prepared two MREs for their supper. When they had finished, Clay pointed out the morning's climb.

"We'll have to backtrack some to avoid the worst part of the seep. Some of the creek trail'll be under water, too, I'd guess. May have to bushwhack part of the way."

"You are sure our fire cannot be seen?" Pablo asked.

"Unless they have posted someone up on the ridge, I'd say no."

"You have referred to 'they' a couple of times now. If Stensvahl is there, does he have company?"

"Sorry. Just a way of staying on top of things, being prepared." John Henry did not understand quite why he did not mention Julie to Pablo. *Why would it make any difference? On the other hand, if Pablo was not all that he claimed to be, what could it hurt?*

They turned in fairly early. Pablo was clearly tired and Clay welcomed the chance to stretch out and rest his knees. He didn't bother with his tent, just spread out the ground cloth and pad, rolled open the sleeping bag and, when he was ready, crawled in. At some point during the night he awoke and got up to relieve himself. As he came back to his bed, he was certain that Pablo was awake and had a gun trained on him. *Well, why not?*

He doesn't know me any better than I know him.

Days 9 & 10

Murder

Morales slipped back twice as they tried to help him to the top of the scramble. When he reached the top the first thing he did was to aim a kick at Ignacio who danced back out of El Coronel's reach. Eddie started to slip back into his pack.

"What are you doing?" demanded Morales.

"Moving out. We can't stay here, this is a flash flood canyon. We have to get out of it." The Tarahumara nodded agreement.

"Nonsense. I go no further. We will camp here." It was obvious that El Coronel Morales was not used to having his judgment questioned.

Eddie looked steadily at the officer. "You stay here, then. I'll meet you at the canyon mouth, assuming you are not washed away during the night."

"You did not hear me. I said *we* will camp here. That includes you," he said acidly.

"Perhaps the good Coronel did not hear *me*. I'm going, Bub, and you can do as you damn well please."

"I will kill you if you take another step," Morales had produced a 9mm pistol and had leveled it at Eddie's chest. "You will stay with us."

Ignacio's response was immediate. Eddie thought later that the actions of Col. Morales triggered something deep down within the Tarahumara; whether the constant insults or the try at kicking him touched him off, or... whatever it was, the result was almost instantaneous. Swinging his hiking staff with all he could muster, Ignacio caught Morales squarely behind the left ear and sent him sprawling half over the edge of the rockfall. As Morales groggily rolled to his right to recover the gun, a return swing of the staff crushed the Federale's left eye socket. He rolled backwards, and over the edge.

As Eddie tried to recover himself, Ignacio was already over the side and working his way down the scramble. Morales was lying in a shallow pool, head partially submerged. The Tarahumara felt his neck, then his wrist. He looked up at Eddie Sam and said simply, *"Muerte."* Dead.

He extracted a document holder from the officer's jacket pocket and from it withdrew a wad of pesos and dollars, and two documents.

Eddie, standing at the top with his hands on his knees, said, "Leave some. Do not make it look like he was robbed."

For a brief moment Ignacio looked puzzled, then he brightened and nodded; after stuffing his own pocket, tucked the folder back into the dead man's jacket. He looked up at Eddie and gave him a half salute.

"Momentito!" Sam grabbed Ignacio's pack, affixed a rope and dropped it carefully to him.

Ignacio looked at Eddie, lips in the hint of a smile, said, *"Adios,"* and started away. Then he turned back and added, *"Buena suerte."* Good luck. He turned on his heel and left.

Eddie Sam struggled to come to grips with what had just taken place. He had watched a murder and a robbery, and he had aided and abetted the fugitive. Well, if not quite murder, something damn close to it. He should climb down and... and what? While Eddie was no stranger to people dying suddenly around him, it was terribly hard to avoid the ingrained Navajo – was it genetic? – distaste for dealing with bodies. Besides that, he told himself, he had his friend's back to watch. He picked up his pack and his staff and walked away, an involuntary shiver running up his back.

Darkness had almost completely taken the canyon mouth when he rolled into his sleeping bag. He could smell a wood fire up-canyon, but could not see it from where he camped. *Tomorrow could be even more interesting,* he thought. Strangely, he had no trouble drifting off to sleep.

The climb was not nearly as easy as Clay remembered it, and it wasn't easy then. Some of the trail just wasn't there, washed away in spring torrents. Rocks, from pea to boulder sized had been moved as if by careless giants. Tracking anyone was impossible and he didn't try. He had paused about three quarters of the way up while he calculated the final bit of climb. He and Pablo had moved far enough from the original track that a false start now could lead them to a blind or to someplace where they would have to spend half the day backtracking. He wasn't worried about Eddie Sam following them. For all he knew, Eddie was within hollering distance now, for they had left an easy trail to for him. Pablo was hanging in there gamely, but he was on his last reserves Clay knew.

He pictured the contours of the terrain in his mind's eye. The valley could be reached climbing roughly as they were; it could be reached via a saddle in the northeast wall of the canyon; and... well, one could come up behind this ridge, then join up with the trail he was now trying to find. Of course, he could consult the little GPS that was tucked into a corner of his pack, but that would be a betrayal of principle. There might be a back way in, but he hesitated to contemplate that climb, and, besides it wouldn't do them any good now. So, find this trail again.

Onward, ever upward, he thought. *Shit.*

Not long after, he cut a game trail leading in the right direction and was soon rewarded by the sight of the notch spewing water in a dozen directions as it sought to escape from the tank. Stepping carefully through a spray of water, they clambered up the remaining several feet to the lip of the pond.

Once again the outright beauty of the place took his breath. The red cliffs, stained with desert varnish and framed by the sky, played background to brook and pond and birds and bloom as did nothing in his past experience. *A man could do worse.*

The two of them crossed the creek, and fairly strolled up and onto the broad bench below what Clay had begun to think of as 'the pueblo cliffs.' There was no scent of a fire, no movement, nothing. Pablo said, "Is this where he is supposed to be?"

"I guess we'll see. This was our only option, you know."

"Alright. Do we make camp? Or is there something else we should be doing?"

"My best guess is, make camp, see what happens. I don't exactly expect him to come running out to shake hands."

As they had mounted the bank, Clay had seen the unmistakable sign of a black bear. Close by was a muddled print that could have been Julie's. The bear had come up onto the bench, then been spooked by the way its tracks veered to the left, back toward the creek. *She's up here, I know it.*

As he had before, Clay popped his tent out in the open but dropped the bedroll to the rear of the camp as though he was just setting it aside for the moment. While Pablo scrounged for wood, John Henry laid a fire about where he had done so in November.

She came in shortly after they finished what passed for their lunch. Her hair was a little wild, otherwise she looked fairly normal. "Hello the fire," she said.

John Henry smiled his little smile, said, "Hello yourself."

Pablo showed neither surprise nor upset. "This is the daughter? Where is Stensvahl?"

"He's not here. I came all this way, but he's not here," she said.

Pablo looked at Clay, and sighed. "She's lying. We can backtrack her, find him."

Clay tugged the end of his mustache. "Mister, she says he's not here. She says it and I believe her." A flat statement, delivered without emotion.

"You can track her in a minute! You know she is lying."

"Mister, I don't recall any agreement between us that said I was to answer your orders. I offered to lead you up here 'cause the girl might be up here. She is. Far as I'm concerned, my part's done."

"All the time we stand here, he could be further away. We are wasting time. How much do you want to track the man?"

"You didn't hear me. My part is this is done. I'm taking the girl back."

Pablo sighed again. "No... no. She does not leave. She is the ticket to her father. I am sure he is watching now to see what we do. We will simply use her." As he was talking, he rummaged in his fanny pack and came out with an ATM .22 mag which he pointed in Clay's general direction. "This is my play now. It will be done as I say. Mr. Clay, please drop your utility belt to the ground – very carefully. Thank you. Now please step away from it."

Clay complied, while mentally searching for a way out.

"Alright, tie the girl up."

John Henry looked bemused. "Aw, come on...you don't want to tie her. Just take her shoes."

"What?"

"Take her shoes. What is she going to do without shoes? She surely can't run anywhere. She'll barely be able to walk on this gravel, especially with all this sharp stuff growing around. Besides, she will be useful if she can move around some."

Pablo took his time considering, the pistol never wavering. "Alright... that makes some sense. You take yours off also."

"Pablo, you want my feet in good shape if I am going to be forced to track someone. My boots stay on."

"Mister Clay, need I remind you which of us has the gun?"

"I don't think that's the question. The real question is how you are going to go about converting this situation into one where you can kill Dub."

"You intrigue me. Explain."

John Henry's brow furrowed. "You come all the way up here into the tulles to kill Dub Stensvahl. That's what you're getting paid for, right? So here you are with no Dub; instead you have an old man and a fifteen year old girl. We are your albatross, so to speak. You weren't hired to do us, but we are in the way. You find him, hell, he can be disposed of and put where he'll never be found. Besides that, who's really gonna care?" He tugged at the 'stache again. "You do us in, gonna be a big stink, they're gonna turn the world over looking for us. Even if you get clean away, your bosses aren't going to like that much."

"So what do you suggest?"

"Why not leave the two of us without shoes? Actually you wouldn't even have to do that. You beat it back to civilization where you wait for us to bring Stensvahl out. You will be at least a day ahead of us."

"Well, Mr. Clay, you make an interesting argument. But I think that there is a much simpler solution. I do away with you, then use the girl for bait." With that he took a step toward Clay and raised his pistol.

Eddie Sam had worked his way carefully toward the lip of the tank. He decided that since he didn't know what John Henry's situation was, no sense in blundering into something. The trail brought him alongside the pond. He could hear nothing over the rushing water; no humans were in sight. He crossed the creek as stealthily as he could, crawled up the bank to where he see onto the bench. What he saw immediately dismayed him.

John Henry and Julie were standing within a few feet of one another, screening Pablo from Eddie. Julie, for some reason holding her boots in her hands. Their backs were toward him. Pablo, facing Eddie, was holding a pistol on both, perhaps a dozen feet from them. The group stood some twenty meters away. Too far to risk a shot with his old Chief's Special, now clutched in Eddie's right hand. *Too far, and I need more line of sight,* he thought. He started to work back to the tank, to try an encircling move to the left.

Eddie had wormed back within 15 or so meters, with the two hostages in the clear. Almost enough to risk a shot... maybe. Just as he was working this in his head, two things happened that brought him to action. The first was when Pablo took a step toward John Henry and raised his weapon to a kill position. The second, which followed almost instantly was a banshee howl raised from Pablo's right.

Pablo reacted. He was astonished, but his years of experience caused him to pivot, gun up, on the sound. He was greeted with "STAND AND DELIVER" from a wraith-like figure stepping from behind a boulder. As he poised, squeezing the trigger, a battering ram hit him squarely in his chest, and then he was on his back seeing blue sky. He tried to focus on the figure and bring the pistol to bear again. The wraith was in a shooter's stance, holding a huge revolver on him. Then his vision closed in on darkness.

Eddie charged onto the scene. Agnes stood with the gun hanging at her side, the other arm around Julie. Clay prodded the dead man with his toe and grunted a greeting to Sam.

All Eddie could say was, "Damn. She saved your ass, son." And then added, "With a Dirty Harry gun at that! Damn!"

Agnes said, "It's my brother-in-law's. I made him loan it to me." She was shaking, Julie holding her tightly.

"Agnes, I gotta ask – where in the world did 'Stand and deliver' come from?"

"John Henry, it was the only thing I could think of when I jumped out there." There were tears in her eyes.

Puerto Palomas

Max Cathcart, The World's Most Inept Drug Dealer, stepped out of the trailer into the fresh air and sunlight, still brilliant even late in the day. The single-wide at one time must have served some venerable service for the Mexican Government; however sometime in its long and varied past it had been pressed into use as the *Oficia Aduana*, Customs Office, at the Palomas crossing. Inside an ancient air conditioner whined but produced little in the way of comfort. The place reeked of stale, smoky air. The officer working the counter had been efficient, if a tad brusque.

He was still smarting from his recent forfeit of some $10,000, lost in the effort to regain entry to the flesh business, and his next check wasn't due for almost a month. He had been churning several ideas that could put him back into some sort of business, most of which involved rather large up-front investment. His business today, renewing his visitor's visa, was done. He was glad to have it over with, business with government was at best tedious, even though they no longer expected the *mordida* payment.

Two middle aged customs agents were nearby, sweating and swearing their way through a series of inspections of south-bound vehicles. From the questions they were asking the occupants, it was obvious to him that they were searching, if half-heartedly, for money and/or weapons. Carrying any sort of firearms or ammunition into Mexico could be dealt with harshly. Max knew that unless one was extremely well connected, someone caught with guns could expect some pretty dismal prison time.

A swirl of pedestrian traffic brushed by him intent on clearing the "downtown" area before nightfall. One person, a tall Tarahumara, almost knocked him off the sidewalk in his haste. He reflected briefly that it was most unusual to see an Indian crossing back from the US side. *Oh, well.*

Max was intrigued at first by the casualness of the inspections being done just a few feet away. Then his agile mind started working. *If I were to want to bring in weapons, I'd damn sure to hide them so these burkes couldn't find them... you could field strip a Kalashnikov and scatter the parts... I wonder how much one of those things is worth down here now... humm...*

Epilog

Eddie took a long pull at his canteen, capped it, and said as if to no one in particular, "Dub's here, isn't he?"

"Pretty good bet."

"I s'pose he's up there in those rocks now, trying to figure out what we are going to do next."

"Prob'ly"

"OK, what tipped you?

John Henry pushed his old Celtics cap back on his head and tugged the end of his mustache. "Julie came out almost right away. I figured that if ol' Dub weren't here, she'd lay back, see what we'd do. Since she showed up right off the bat, I figure she was trying to stall our hunt. You?"

"He left tracks. Tried to bluff with the old burlap wrap, but since it couldn't be anyone else..."

"Yeah."

Clay and Sam had retreated to the meager shade offered by the part of a rockfall near the cliff. Eddie was sprawled with his back against the rock, Clay sat on his stool off to one side. The late afternoon sun was occasionally hidden for a few moments by puffballs of convection, moving slowly to the east. They had taken temporary refuge while Wanda, aided by Izzy, took statements from the two women.

Eddie Sam said, "Big Bad Wanda says we have 'precipitated at least one international incident'."

"Another fine mess you've gotten us into."

"Where have I heard that before? She say anything about the follow-up on this?"

"Only that we were stuck here until the law can straighten it out. Maybe day after tomorrow."

"I s'pose we'll be tripping over the press guys."

"I don't think so... Eddie, I'll bet this gets swept under somebody's rug. We have a dead Mexican Federal – at least we *think* he was Federal – who had no business here to begin with. We have a dead international assassin. Dub is not officially here. Wanda's going to be reassigned in a day or two. It's the Fed's worry now; don't sweat it."

"Maybe I'll go back to the Big Res and push some sheep around for a while."

They sat quietly for several minutes.

Finally, Clay looked over at Eddie. "Tell me something. What was the 'Dirty Harry' thing?"

Eddie said, "Take a look at that revolver. It's an S&W Model 29, .44 mag, four inch barrel, just like in the movie. It'd blow away an elephant."

High overhead the puffy convection clouds rolled from canyon wall to canyon wall, the sun a brilliant disc peeking between them.

John Henry broke the silence. "Did you think that Morales was one of the bad guys?"

"John Henry, I still don't know if he was or not. He treated that Indian like shit, but..." and he let it hang. "How 'bout you? When did you figure out that Pablo wasn't what he said he was?"

"I figured as much after I got a call from Cap'n Eddie. He caught me even before we got to Deming. Said he'd seen him hanging with Don Benito at the airport. Said he thought maybe I ought to know."

"Uh huh."

Clouds were chasing clouds across New Mexico's famous blue sky. Eddie fanned away a fly.

"Say, Hoss, I been thinkin'"

"Uh-oh."

"Seriously, Big Guy. What would you think – as a purely academic exercise..."

"Purely."

"...Yeah, purely as an academic exercise, of us... ah... in

the pursuit of our professional..."

"Very professional."

"Well, yeah... as an exercise in professional practice, as it were..."

"Practice."

"Dammit, John Henry, if you are going to keep interrupting..."

"Oh, sorry, I was just absorbing, so to speak."

"Yeah, right. How long would it take us – as a purely academic exercise, as I said – to pick up Dub's trail and..."

"Find his gold source?"

"Well... yeah."

"How long we got?"

"Wouldn't take that long." Eddie scanned the sky as if seeking answers. "Even if we don't find track, and probably won't after this long, process of elimination..."

"Absolutely."

After a long pause, Clay said, "I suppose that if you were to refuse to spend the night here in the canyon with a dead body on strictly ethno-religious grounds..."

"Ethno-religious."

"...I could volunteer to keep you company and safe from any nasty skinwalker..."

"Oh, nasty, nasty skinwalker..."

"...we might, speculatively speaking..."

"Speculatively."

"...enter into the kind of enterprise you have in mind. We could probably steal half a day or so out from under Ranger Brubaker's watchful eye."

Hidden in the rocks at the rim of the canyon, a figure sat huddled, arms around his knees, head down. To his left, peering into the valley, the Reverend Orville Foss shook his head. "I 'spect that was a close one. You know, Mister Dub Stensvahl, it's gonna take them a few days to get all this mess cleaned up and sorted. What say, you and me, we talk a little more about this gold strike of yours..."

If you have enjoyed *Tracking Julie Stensvahl* Bill invites you to have a sneak peek at his next Tracking adventure.

Tracking Jesus Garza

By Bill Wehner

Prologue

Spain, Late Summer 1997

He let the Fiat roll the last few feet into the car park to the side of Malaga's Hotel Maestranza. Dadaian was tired, he was sweaty, and he needed a drink. First, however, he had to make a phone call. He slipped easily out of the car and walked toward the lobby. Dadaian was of average size and average build, he could have been from anywhere in Europe or even parts of the Middle East. His light tan slacks and short sleeved blue sport shirt were off-the-rack from a clothier in Marbella. He was in his late thirties or perhaps early forties and his dark hair was beginning to thin in front. His loafers were scuffed but serviceable; in short, he was not someone you would notice, and if you did, he'd soon be forgotten.

He headed straight for the phone bank at the rear of the lobby. He made the call from memory, charging it to his phone card. The lobby clock read 1708, or 5:08 PM. The phone rang twice before being picked up. A woman's voice said, *"Hola?"*

"Senora Munoz, this Dadaian. How are you this afternoon?"

In Spanish, she replied, "Oh, Señor Dadaian, it is so good to hear from you." She was almost gushing. "I had expected you yesterday... I made a lamb stew. But it will be just as good tonight."

He had rented rooms from Señora Muñoz for almost a year and a half now, and was in the habit of calling an hour or so before each return. He was in Malaga now, near the city's Plaza del Toros, and her tiny village was only about 30 minutes away. Why he had let himself get so close this evening before stopping to call he didn't know.

She was rattling on, "...and my sister, you know, Maria, the tall one? Well, she has had little but trouble with that stupid car..." He listened politely for several minutes, then asked the same question he always asked, "Did I have any callers?"

She took that to mean, did he have any telephone calls? She replied in the negative, as she usually did, then hesitated. He caught the hesitation. Was there something else?"

"Well, she wanted it to be a surprise, she asked me not to say anything until she had a chance to stop back to see you. She said she had something for you, but she wanted to deliver it herself." Certainly one of the advantages of renting from Señora Muñoz was that she was a font of gossip who could not keep anything to herself if her life depended on it.

"I am intrigued. Please tell me about her."

"Ah, Señor Dadaian, she was very plain. I would not of thought her your type at all. I thought that perhaps she was one of those tall, stodgy Americans that stop here every now and then, but she spoke good Madrid Spanish and she was well dressed in a stodgy way."

To himself, he wondered what type would be his, or if he even had a type. Aloud, he asked, "How old? Hair color?"

"Let me see... ah...light hair, not blonde, but light. How old? Well, maybe just a little younger than I. Late forties, maybe."

My Dear, he thought, you haven't seen the late forties since I was a babe... Aloud, he asked, "Anything else about her strike you? She doesn't sound like someone I know."

There was a pause before she offered: "She was driving a Fiat just like yours except it was light blue."

"No... doesn't ring a bell. Well. Oh, before I forget to tell you – I called to let you know that I won't be in tonight. The main office just called me, they have a job for me up the coast... I probably will not be back for several days. Unfortunately, that means I will miss your wonderful stew, at least for now."

After murmuring further apologies, he hung up. I should call Ari, he thought. But first, a drink and then dinner. Señora Muñoz put the phone in its cradle thoughtfully. Señor Dadaian was, she supposed, a strange man. She thought that she had gotten to know him fairly well since he took up lodgings, but if she were to be honest with herself, she realized that she knew little about him. Because of his name, she supposed that he was of Armenian extraction, and although he talked from time to time about various places in France and Germany, she had not a single clue about his origin. He had gently refused to get beyond the handshake stage with any of the widows who 'happened' to drop in on Señora Muñoz – in fact, her sister (the short one) had simply stated that Señor Dadaian was most certainly queer. He spoke good Spanish, perhaps with a bit of a middle European accent, and her sister (the one who worked in the Marbella hotel) assured her that his English made him sound sort of American. The good senora had heard him on the telephone conversing in what she assumed to be German or Dutch and once had heard him cursing in some language that was totally unfamiliar to her.

Not that she thought that his facility in language was at all strange, for she got along in three herself and her late husband (God keep him) spoke Italian, Basque, and French, and was able to get by in Portuguese, English, and a little Arabic. No, that wasn't it. Senor Dadaian seemed to have no interests beyond his job, whatever that was, and kept pretty much to himself. Oh well.

Dadaian was disturbed by his conversation. Señora Muñoz said the woman had spoken with a Madrid accent, whatever that was. Did she mean Castilian? He doubted that the Senora herself had ever been anywhere near Madrid, let alone be able to recognize an accent from that rather cosmopolitan city. By Mediterranean standards it was quite early for the last meal of the day, but he was hungry, he decided, and he needed to let things simmer in his head. He took a table in the restaurant and ordered a green salad and a filet, poured himself a glass of the local rioja and thought about what Senora Munoz had told him. The woman had driven up in a light blue Fiat, a late model like his own, and asked for him by name. Since no one knew – or was supposed to know – where he lived, he must have been recognized somewhere and then followed. Her appearance on his door step was amateurish... or at least meant to appear that way. Only Avram knew where he was planning to go to ground, but there was no way of knowing what name he would be using. No matter – the immediate question was: should he activate Plan B? Or was the woman merely an instrument that was supposed to start him running?

If only Avram were still alive. He was the planner of all planners; he taught us to follow his three rules. After each mission we'd each have to justify our actions based on those rules: (A) observe and understand everything happening or about to happen around you; (B) adapt to the situation; (C) look for the simplest solution, always. Situational awareness; go with the flow; keep it simple, stupid – Avram's laws of survival. They had always worked in the past, but now he had major decisions to make.

Someone had made him. Therefore, it was probable that more than one person knew his identity and location by now – probably several more. That they seemed to be interested in frightening him into running instead of just taking him was interesting. Did they hope he would lead them to some of his benefactors? Or were they just intent on seeing what he would do, where he would run?

If he ran... he would stop being Dadaian, he would leave Spain entirely, he would adopt an entirely new persona; he would become a new person. Not that he wasn't ready to do just that. Avram had insisted that there always be a 'Plan B' and that a 'Plan C' be ready as well. OK, he had both plans ready to implement even if this was rather short notice. The real question (and the only one, really) was: should I do it now?

They must have watchers on him; someone here in this room, someone else watching the car, maybe. If they hadn't taken him by now it was odds-on that he would have at least a few more weeks of freedom, maybe a few more weeks of life. He was not especially afraid of dying; he just didn't want to do it now. He had told Senora Munoz that he wouldn't be back for several days. If indeed they were watching him – and he had to assume that they were – then he must not do anything to alert them to whatever decision he must make. Go with the flow. Thank you, Avram.

He took his time with his supper, finishing with a cup of coffee, while poring over a day-old Paris Match. Finally, he stubbed out his cigarette, discarded the paper and walked out to his car. He had filled the tank that afternoon on the way back from Alicante, so petrol was not a consideration. Whatever was left with Señora Muñoz, well, she could have. There certainly wasn't much. Time was on his side, too, he could board the morning ferry and be in Tangier tomorrow for the midday meal. He relaxed as he reached the eastern outskirts of Malaga and turned on to the coast highway.

He kept his speed between 75 and 80 kph on the limited access, but did not notice anyone that seemed interested in him. The sun set on him as he passed through Torremolinos; glimpses of the Mediterranean revealed an inky blue with fiery red accents as the heat of the afternoon began to give way to the slight chill of evening. He left behind Fuengirola, Marbella and Estepania. Gibraltar loomed in the distance. At San Roque, in the shadow of the great monolith, he found a small pension and turned in for the night after requesting a 0530 call.

In the morning, Dadaian arose, took a quick shower (pleasantly surprised that the water was actually hot), ate a croissant with a cup of coffee, retrieved the Fiat and headed south on the A-7, the *"Autovia del Mediterraneo."* At Algeciras, he turned left onto Avenida Virgen del Carmine for the short distance to the municipal docks. He parked in roughly the middle of the ferry landing car park. After purchasing a ticket (one way) he sat in the waiting area, drinking more coffee. The dawn had been spectacular, promising a storm before nightfall, but the crossing this morning looked to be uneventful. While he did not scan the gathering crowd as carefully as he might have under other circumstances, he did not see anyone who seemed to be a watcher.

He had always enjoyed deck passage on the huge ferry, especially Friday and Sunday evenings when the Moroccan students and laborers were either returning to Spain or going home for the weekend. There would be music and laughter, and the deck would be thick with the scent of weed and sweat. It was quiet this morning. He made his way to the café and ordered a soft drink. After all these years it still was a slight shock to pick up a Coke bottle that was worn translucent through repeated bottling and was printed with Arabic lettering. He thought about his situation. He had money, not the millions he'd like, but enough to carry him into a ripe old age with a fair amount of comfort. He planned to go to ground in Tangier; he'd laid the ground work to use that city as an intermediate stop several years ago. That he could not stay in Tangier, though, was a given. Following Avram's strategy, he had set up three or four possible bolt-holes but the kicker was how to get to them from Tangier. He set his mind to those possibilities.

He had finally ruled out New Zealand, as much as he admired that lovely country, leaving three others to consider. Actually, there were few places he could call home by just fading into the woodwork, so to speak. Dadian had seriously thought about a few large cities he might retreat to, then ruled out an urban existence. He felt that he needed to live off the grid, somewhere he could spot danger before it came at him, at the same time be unnoticed against the background. Someplace fairly isolated, perhaps, with a back door or two. Yes, live off the grid... yet be able to avail himself of it at important times. He needed to access his banks, he needed to be a fairly average, law abiding, unnoticed citizen.

These last seven or eight years he had, of necessity, lived a fairly monastic existence. Almost celibate, now that he thought about it. A man in his profession does not develop relationships no matter how casual, whatever Ian Fleming's hero James Bond might do.

For the last two years, since he had decided to free-lance and cut himself loose from his former employer, he had played it so very close to the vest, he almost couldn't believe that he'd slipped up and allowed himself to be found. Oh, well, he thought, that's certainly water over the dam.

After disembarking from the ferry, he spent a part of the morning's remainder at the marketplace just above the docks, and ate couscous at a small café. He then wandered up into the fabled Kasbah district, pausing several times to inspect merchandise at the closet sized shops that lined the street. He seemed, for all the world, like a businessman on a brief holiday, enjoying himself and passing the time of day with the tradesmen in Arabic, English and Spanish.

The Kasbah occupies the highest quarter of Tangier and is walled off from the rest of the Tangier, a city within a city. A large court lays just inside its gate, facing Dar el-Makhzem, the old sultan's palace, now a museum. The Kasbah itself has a public face, a tourist face along each narrow street and alley, with walls consisting of homes turning their blind side to the public passageways, punctured by closed doors and accented by the open doors of the tiny stalls of street merchants. Behind those walls, private luxurious gardens and lush dwellings stood cheek-by-jowl with rat infested tenements. Viewed from above, the quarter was a rabbit warren spilling down the hillside to the harbor, punctuated by TV antennas.

Dadaian sampled wares from a dozen stalls, and actually made a few purchases as he worked his way up hill, deeper into the quarter. He selected a *Kaftan* and a couple of *djellabas* from one clothier. The watcher stationed closer to him (the one who had picked him out of the crowd on the Algeciras docks) carefully noted their style and pattern. He observed Dadaian make a series of left and right turns as he ambled upwards through the maze. His quarry now turned to his right and strolled down a very narrow alley. There were only a half dozen doors piercing the walls on either side, none of them open. A little over halfway down the block, Dadaian suddenly turned to his right, reached for the handle of one of the closed doors, opened it quickly, slipped inside and closed the door behind him. His watcher had not yet followed him into the alley for fear of being spotted and stood rooted for a second before deciding to act.

Watchers by nature (at least the good ones) are not impetuous creatures, nor are they necessarily gifted with a huge amount of imagination, and this one took several seconds to decide what to do. At last, he sprinted to the doorway where he had last seen his quarry, twisted the handle and cautiously opened it. He was greeted by an even more constricted alleyway, and a mass of doorways opening to tenements or to stairways to tenements. Dadaian was nowhere to be seen.

In the city of Tel Aviv, Ari ben Kemmel approached the desk of Mikos Constanaeides.

"He's gone," he stated without expression.

"Surprised?" was the retort.

"I guess not. His landlady said he'd had a woman looking for him, and that he hadn't been back, and that she hadn't heard from him. She did have his auto license number. His car is in the ferry car park in Algeceras, empty. He either went to Tangier, or wanted the world to think he did."

"Any idea who the woman was?"

"The question is, who wants to chat with him... or wanted to spook him into taking off like that."

"Well, Ari, do you think he will turn up, or do you suppose he's decided to retire."

Ari ben Kemmel dragged deeply on his cigarette before answering. "I think he was getting tired of it all when he decided to freelance. He and Avram were very close... I think when Avram was lost, he made a decision then. Who knows?"

Mikos thought, where does a Sabra assassin run to when he runs? Aloud, he said, "He'll turn up in dumpster somewhere." Then added, "He's a funny guy, though, he might be able to just shut down and avoid damage. Maybe."

Kemmel made a wry face and hesitated a moment before he offered, "If you were in his shoes...?"

The question hung there. Constanaeides just shook his head.

Over the next several months, the office received reports of Dadaian being spotted in Tunis, Paris, Dublin, Barcelona, Nice, and Brest. None of the reports proved productive, although had they been able to follow up the Barcelona sighting, they might have discovered that a slight man very much resembling Dadaian had shipped out as a steward on a cruise liner using documents that were only partially counterfeit.

CPSIA information can be obtained at www.ICGtesting.com

224547LV00004B/1/P